DANGER BOY

—— Trail of Bones ——

Mark London Williams

CANDLEWICK PRESS
CAMBRIDGE, MASSACHUSETTS

This is a work of fiction. Names, characters, places,
and incidents are either products of the author's imagination
or, if real, are used fictitiously.

Copyright © 2005 by Mark London Williams
Danger Boy®. Danger Boy is a registered trademark of Mark London Williams.

First paperback edition 2007

The Library of Congress has cataloged the hardcover edition as follows:
Williams, Mark London.
Trail of bones / Mark London Williams. —1st ed.
p.   cm. — (Danger boy)
Summary: Time travelers Eli and Thea arrive in Missouri in 1804,
where they meet Thomas Jefferson and other famous people,
then Eli joins the Corps of Discovery, hoping to find Clyne so
that the three friends can return to the Fifth Dimension.
ISBN 978-0-7636-2154-4 (hardcover)
[1. Time travel—Fiction. 2. Jefferson, Thomas, 1743–1826—Fiction.
3. Hemings, Sally—Fiction. 4. Lewis and Clark Expedition
(1804–1806)—Fiction. 5. Slavery—Fiction. 6. Science fiction.]
I. Title.
PZ7.W66697Tr 2005
[Fic] —dc22   2004056130

ISBN 978-0-7636-3410-0 (paperback)

2 4 6 8 10 9 7 5 3 1

Printed in the United States of America

This book was typeset in Slimbach Book.

Candlewick Press
2067 Massachusetts Avenue
Cambridge, Massachusetts 02140

visit us at www.candlewick.com

This one's for Becky and Caitlin,
the earliest members of my own
"Corps of Discovery."

Prologue

They shake the boy, call his name. "Eli! Eli!" They can't tell yet if he's still alive.

The boy is poked and prodded. When his eyes open a little, there's a surge of relief. The boy was dreaming of lying in a sunny field, of waking to warmth and friendship. If the search party hadn't come along, perhaps he'd have kept dreaming forever, lying in the field of snow where his rescuers found him.

The search party is made up of explorers, U.S. Army captains, a shaman from a local Indian tribe— journeyers of every sort. Including a young Indian woman—not really all that much older than the boy— named Sacagawea.

Sacagawea is married to a fur trapper and has wandered around the plains and mountains a lot, and she's pretty sure her wandering days aren't over yet. But she's always come through okay.

She considers herself lucky.

She wonders if this young man considers himself lucky, too. He must. What else would he be doing out here by himself?

She knows the reasons they gave at the fort, when they were heading out to look for him: that he'd headed out for the Spirit Mound — a hill that was supposed to be haunted not only by spirits and phantoms but, lately, by a lizard who walks upright like a man. And even talks.

Those were the whispered stories.

And the boy was trying to get there, alone, on foot, the whispers went, to reach the lizard man. It was said they had some kind of connection.

Sacagawea also feels a small, growing connection to this young man, this Eli, since she was the first to find him.

She is good at reading signs, good at picking up trails. When she heard there was a search party heading out, she insisted on being part of it. Her husband, the fur trapper, always more cautious than she, tried to forbid her going. She was, after all, thick with child, ready to give birth very soon. And for a lot of men in her place and time, a pregnant woman wasn't good luck at all — just the opposite.

But her fur-trapper husband also knew she was a better tracker than he was, so when word came that the boy had left on his own, with another snowstorm coming, and she insisted on going, the forbiddance lasted only a few minutes.

He was worried about the baby, but then again, how long would they really be gone? How far could the boy have gotten?

Pretty far, as it turned out.

The boy had put together a route from the Spirit Mound stories—many from the same young shaman who now helped look for him—and struck out to see his friend. For his part, the fur trapper agreed with most of the exploring party that stories about the walking, talking lizard man were nonsense. How could such a creature exist?

But Sacagawea kept an open mind.

She'd seen the boy around the fort, overheard his conversations a lot, and liked him. He seemed to be like she was, an outsider, a person from somewhere else, who found himself on a journey not of his own making, but who was a good traveler, anyway.

"Wake up," she said in her people's tongue to the near-frozen boy, as everyone stood around, watching his eyelids flutter and his unfocused eyes trying to make sense of where he was. "Come back to us."

Instead, the boy closed his eyes again and dreamed of the sunny field.

Perhaps the same sunny field where President Jefferson and the others had found him last spring.

"We have found you now," the Indian woman tells the boy. "You can come back to this world. You will be all right."

"Sacagawea?" The others stand close, near where she found the boy nestled by the crook of a storm-shattered tree. "Is he all right?"

It's the one named Lewis who's asking her. His partner, Clark, the coleader of the explorers, stayed behind at the fort. Lewis shakes Eli a little and gets a smile, but it's a bit of a vacant smile, and the boy still doesn't quite wake up.

Sacagawea knows what it's like to be in one place and dream of another.

She dreams of her own home, with her tribe, the Shoshones. Dreams of the time before she was kidnapped as a girl, then sold to other tribes or, eventually, in the case of her husband, Charbonneau, to another man.

Lately, she's had this strong feeling that she might be seeing her home again, for the first time in years.

Perhaps all the boy really wanted was to go home.

"E—li?" she says, trying his name out loud.

Her hand closes around the stone she wears next to her skin—the one that her brother, the chief's son, gave her the day she was taken. A stone that was supposed to be passed along from chief to chief, a talisman she now wears for luck and protection.

She'd had the rock with her ever since. When you've been captured and sold, you know a little about the world. The stone—the jagged crystal—has warmed her, kept her steady through all the twists and turns.

She knows the boy's journey isn't supposed to end yet. He isn't supposed to stay asleep in the snow.

"Come on, Eli!" Another man from the fort. Named Gass.

"Stay. Here." And North Wind Comes, the shaman-to-be from the Mandan people, neighbors of the very Hidatsas who sold her to Charbonneau.

Sacagawea lifts the leather strap from around her neck.

She presses the stone into the boy's hands. His

fingers are really cold, almost too cold to move, but she gets them to shut around the stone, and puts her own hands around his.

"Sacagawea, we need to get him back." It's Charbonneau, talking to her in that slightly alarmed way he has around her, especially when she's making her own decisions.

"Wait," she says to all of them, again speaking in the Shoshone she hasn't used in far too long.

For a moment, it seems the boy might fall asleep again, and Sacagawea knows that would be bad, to let him return to slumber in the cold like this. Even dreaming of sunny fields wouldn't help.

But then his eyelids stay open and the eyes beneath them glisten and come into focus at last.

"Th-th-thank you," he says through chattering teeth, the warmth coming now not from his dreams, but from the rock in his hand.

Sacagawea gives him a little smile, then nods.

The boy will be all right.

She feels a little kick inside her stomach.

There are other journeys yet to come. For all of them.

Chapter One

"Well, he's certainly not a giant."

"And he ain't no Indian, either. I don't think."

"What shall we do with him, Mr. Jefferson?"

All this talking. It makes my head hurt. It's like the time I fell asleep on the couch during one of my parents' parties, and I still remember hearing the phrase *brain universe* as I was being picked up off the sofa to be put to bed.

I was five and I thought of colossal-sized brains until the time I found out it was spelled "brane" and meant something else entirely, about the way the whole universe — and maybe the universes around it, or next to it — are designed.

The design of my own universe used to be better: There was no jarring time travel, no vanished parents, no talking dinosaurs to explain.

Well, wait. Not that I want the dinosaur to go away.

It feels sunny and bright above me . . . hot. And cold and damp underneath me.

I'm sweating and I'm rolling around in mud and my own "brain universe" — the one in my head — is aching. I think I'm sick.

But everyone around me is still talking.

"I am not 'Mr. Jefferson' while I am on this trip, Mr. Howard. I am not 'Mr. President.' I am not in charge, and I am not even officially here. Captain Lewis and Captain Clark are in command. I am merely an interested citizen, here to pursue a little science and to wish them well."

I'd better open my eyes and find out who's sounding like some kind of English teacher.

Not English teachers, as it turns out. Cowboys.

Or maybe not cowboys, exactly. Daniel Boone . . . sorts of guys. In scuffed buckskins and leather jackets and raccoon caps and floppy wide hats that look almost like sombreros.

Along with a few other guys in soldier clothes that look like they came from a production of *The Nutcracker,* dressed in long blue coats and boots, bearing guns with pointy bayonets.

One of those guys is taller than the others. He's not quite dressed like a soldier — but he still looks like something from an old painting. With pants that don't go all the way down and stockings and shoes with big buckles. He has a notebook, instead of a gun, and red hair pulled back in a little pony-tail. Hair like one of the hippies I've seen in the history books.

I'd look around, but my "brain universe" — and all the other parts of my head — feel like they weigh a ton.

I turn my neck a little and can see some horses and knapsacks and wooden wagons and long rifles in saddle holsters or dangling from the arms of some of the men.

Thea and Clyne aren't here.

I hope they made it out of the Fifth Dimension. I hope they're okay.

I can hear a river nearby. I guess that explains the mud.

"Mr. Floyd! Have your men tend to the keelboat and mind how they load the crates! We can't afford to lose any provisions before we've even begun!"

Whoever's speaking now has dark hair and dark eyes that you can't see all the way into.

All these boats and provisions and guns. Maybe it's some kind of war party, or patrol. Or expedition.

I try to sit up again, to say something. But my mouth feels like some of the sun and the mud are at war in there, too. Only a gurgling sound comes out.

"Aye-aye, Cap'n Lewis. I'll go down and give them what for." It's one of the cowboy-looking men, in smelly leather, with a stubbly beard and a kind of Civil War costume hat. He leans in and touches my forehead. "The boy seems awful hot."

The man takes a canteen, a leather canteen, from around his shoulder, and he pours a few drops of water on my face.

I realize how thirsty I am.

I try to ask for more, but suddenly, I realize what this feeling is: It's like the moment you come out of a dream but aren't fully awake, and some part of you knows you're not sleeping anymore, but your body isn't ready to start taking any orders yet, either.

Though I wonder, since I travel through time with a talking dinosaur and a girl who's well over a thousand years old, if I'm even in the coming-out-of-a-dream stage at all.

"Let me see him." A taller man, with no hat, leans over the stubble-beard guy, and stares right at me, then opens my eye real wide with his finger and thumb.

"Ow!"

That came out clear enough.

"Least it ain't yellow fever. You American? Or you just lost?"

He's the first one to ask me a direct question.

"I'm—" Before I can find out whether I'm up to speaking a complete sentence, I'm cut off.

"Thank you, York. And you, too, Mr. Floyd. That will be enough for now."

The man with the dark piercing eyes waves

the two of them away. I notice his buckskin jacket is a lot cleaner than the other ones—like maybe his really did come from a costume shop.

"I'm Eli Sands." My words were kind of croaked out, but like the *ow,* you could hear them.

"Well, young Master Sands. Then allow me to introduce myself. I am Captain Meriwether Lewis. Down on the boats somewhere is Captain William Clark. We are setting out on a journey that is probably foolhardy or maybe even suicidal. Perhaps you are foolhardy, as well, to be out here all alone. Or perhaps you are some kind of omen." He follows the word *omen* with a tiny little smile.

The redheaded hippie in the costume comes closer, too, staring at me the way a doctor or dentist might do it.

"Never mind reading the will of heaven, Captain Lewis. Perhaps there's a simpler explanation. Perhaps the boy is an *incognitum.*" He laughs, so maybe it's a joke, but I feel like my own brain universe is about to explode. An *incog*-what?

"And this," Lewis says, nodding toward the ponytailed redhead, "is Mr. Thomas Jefferson."

Thomas Jefferson? Wasn't he—?

"Mr. President! Sir!" A really sweaty man pushes his way next to Jefferson. His *Nutcracker* clothes are more torn up, and he wears a couple extra pistols strapped to his body. "Maybe he's a French or British spy, sir! Maybe the Spanish sent him!"

"Then they're doing a fairly poor job of sneaking up on us, Mr. Howard. And wasn't it your idea that we not refer to me as president while we're on this little jaunt?"

The pistol-wearer's eyes bulge a little more. "Yes, Mr. President. Sorry, sir. This should remain a secret mission."

"This is kind of a big group to be called 'secret.'" It's York. I can hear other voices, and the noise of horses and work. He's right—there seem to be a lot of people here.

"We're not taking advice from some darky slave!" Mr. Howard snaps back.

Darky slave? York is black, it's true. But what kind of awful words—

Where am I? When is this?

"Stand down, Mr. Howard," Jefferson says.

"But he just contradicted—"

"I said, 'Stand down.' Stop shouting at the less fortunate. I'm sure this journey shall stay secret. After all, it's not as if news of the president's travels can fly through thin air."

It's time for me to shake out all the grogginess and find out where I am.

"Um, sir—"

Instead, I throw up. One of those empty-stomach throw-ups that are sometimes the worst.

"The boy's sick."

Don't ever let anyone tell you that time travel is easy.

"Maybe we better take him to St. Louis," the one named Floyd says.

"Portents and omens, sir," Lewis says to Jefferson.

"Let us take him to my camp first," Jefferson says. "It's closer, and Sally can look after him."

I don't want to be *looked after.* I just want to go home.

I'm handed a rag for my mouth.

"Drink this." Floyd holds out some kind of

wooden cup. He decides to help me and tips the liquid into my lips.

Whatever it is — medicine? — it stings and burns, and I start coughing, so thanks to being "helped," I never get the word *no* out of my mouth, as in "No, I don't want to go. I want to stay here and look for my friends —"

But now I'm being led away, my arm around Floyd's shoulder, and he's taking me toward some kind of wooden wagon.

"Up here, little friend."

I'm still not sure where I am, but I'll take the ride, so I let him help me up.

I climb on, and in the rear of the wagon, I see a blanket in the corner that's been thrown over some stuff, so I take it and pull it off.

There's a giant bone underneath it.

Like a dinosaur bone.

Like a bigger-than-Clyne dinosaur bone.

I'm shivering, but I don't put the blanket on.

"Master Sands?" Two men are walking toward the wagon. At least I hope it's two — maybe I'm seeing double. It looks like Jefferson has split into two separate lanky redheaded men.

Except the other one doesn't have a ponytail.

"Are you brothers?" I finally manage to croak out.

Jefferson laughs and turns to the other guy. "Sometimes, Captain Clark, you'd think we were the only two red-haired men in creation, the way people keep asking that. No, young sir,"—and now he's looking at me again—"this is Captain William Clark, the other leader of this noble, somewhat secret, perhaps misbegotten, expedition. You should put the blanket on, Master Sands. I'm sure the bony remains of the *incognitum* won't miss it."

"Before you return to camp, Mr. President, here's the other find you inquired about—the strange hat we found by the riverbank." Clark lifts a sword—a sword! (but it's smaller than Excalibur, and obviously someone besides King Arthur and Thea can hold this one) — and hanging off the tip is my Seals cap.

I grab for the cap without thinking. Without the ship, it's my only chance to get home, and maybe to find my friends.

"Perhaps it belongs to the boy?" Clark asks. Yeah, perhaps it does.

Jefferson takes it from the sword tip to look at it, then drops it as if he's been burned. He squats down to study it. "I should hope not. He'd scald himself. You have found the first scientific anomaly of your long journey, Mr. Clark. An entirely different kind of *incognitum*—a mysterious type of half hat, with lettering on it," he says, pointing to the overlapping *S* and *F*.

That weird word again. What is this *incognitum* that Jefferson is so worked up about?

"You and your *incognitums,* sir." Clark shakes his head. "I appreciate your accompanying us all the way through Missouri in order to look for large and mysterious bones, but let's not terrify the men any more than we have to." Clark pats the bone laying near me on the wagon.

"Dinosaur bone," I tell them, getting a couple more words out of my mouth.

"What?"

"From a *dinosaur.* But not the one who does homework. Luckily."

Clark looks at Jefferson and shrugs. "I don't know what he's saying. Maybe he *is* from another country."

"Dinosaur." Jefferson repeats the word. "It's some kind of Latin I've never heard before."

"Hat."

"What?"

"Hat," I repeat.

I want my Seals cap. Still feeling shaky, I start to reach for it again, thinking I'll climb down from the wagon.

But before I can, I'm jerked back in as the horse the wagon's hitched to starts to move.

"Let Sally tend him!" Jefferson says to the driver of the wagon. "Later, when he's regained his strength, we shall find out how our young squire came to be by the banks of the Ohio River this sunny day in May!"

I'm shivering and still feeling sick, and this time I take the blanket completely off the dinosaur bone and wrap it around myself.

The wagon pulls me along, farther and farther from the baseball cap that's my only real ticket home.

Chapter Two

Thea: Runaway

May 1804

I'm still not sure where I am, but wherever it is, they keep telling me I am a slave. That, at least, is the translation, courtesy of the lingo-spot behind my ear. And *slave,* unfortunately, is one of those words with few alternate meanings.

There was a blackout period after the lizard man K'lion's ship seemed to come alive and spin out of control on our way back from seeing the wizard Merlin and his king, Arthur, and saving the king's cursed-and-weighty blade, Excalibur. The three of us were then separated as we were flung through the Fifth Dimension.

But Eli is here now. I have seen him.

They brought him into camp a short while ago. He appears to be sick.

I wonder if they told him that he's a slave, too?

I haven't been able to get near him, to ask him any questions. But at least we've been pulled toward the same place, the same moment in time.

But which moment? And is our lizard friend nearby?

After the blackout, I awoke in a fairly dense stand of trees, clothing torn, my skin scratched. Working my way through the trees, toward the sound of water, I soon came to a road, or broad path, that appeared to follow the course of a great river.

I drank from the river, cleaned myself as best I could, and eventually heard a group of travelers approaching.

I spied them from the safety of the trees. Since it was a mixed company, both men and women, I decided to show myself.

"Help! Please."

I said it in Latin first. If this was indeed the same Earth that Eli and I know, the Roman language is the most common tongue. At least, it was when I lived there.

"Halt."

The speaker was a tall man, with red hair and somewhat stern, though lively, features. He was riding on a horse. His name, I quickly learned, was Jefferson.

With his raised hand, the horses and pair of wagons behind him pulled to a stop.

Another man, Howard, rode up on another steed and eyed me intensely. "Sir," he said. "I believe that's her."

"Who?"

"The escaped slave from New Orleans. The one whose likeness is featured in all the handbills. Brassy."

Without waiting for a reply, Howard jumped off his horse and grabbed me. "You're coming with us, girl. We'll get you back to your rightful master!"

"Mr. Howard—"

"I have no master!" I used Latin again. The tall redhead looked at me curiously.

The one called Howard was squeezing my wrists. I was getting ready to kick him.

"Mr. *Howard*—"

"What? *Ow!*"

I delivered the blow, but still he held me.

"She speaks Latin."

"It makes no difference, sir—Stop that! Whether she's an overeducated house slave—Ow! Be still!—or a field hand, we must return her. She belongs to the governor of your new territory, sir! You're the president of the United States! You cannot be perceived as helping runaway slaves! *Ow!*"

Jefferson looked away. He appeared to be embarrassed.

"She's just a Negro, sir. A darky. She's no business of the president's."

"No. She is some business of the president's, Mr. Howard. But what sort? That is what we grapple with."

A woman who appeared to be Nubian, or an Ethiop, from the very heart of Africa, sat on top of the largest wagon—a kind of chariot with inner seating and doors—holding the reins of the horses. She stared down at the men. Her eyes were ablaze, but she said nothing.

Jefferson's eyes stayed averted, but he spoke. "And when did you switch from worrying about my security to worrying about politics?"

"Sir—stop that, young wench, or I'll lash you myself!—one should not try to separate security and politics."

Jefferson sighed, finally turning back to face us. He seemed wearier. "No shackles, at least, Mr. Howard. Not for a young girl like that. We'll bring her with us."

Thus was I mistaken for someone's slave. Even after pointing out that *I* approached *them*. I spoke in Latin, and Jefferson translated for his assistant, Howard.

"A ruse," Howard called it. Jefferson was again silent. And so they believe—or wish—me to be an escapee named Brassy.

There were slaves in Alexandria, though mother and I certainly never kept any at the library. But many of the wealthier families had them. Mother argued against the idea of slavery, in a lecture, once. Another reason a lot of people hated her.

In Alexandria, slavery was a function of

economics—or a failure of it. People would often sell themselves as slaves if they had no other means of support.

But usually it's about more than just money. Like at Peenemünde, the rocket factory of the Third Reich, where K'lion and I were taken prisoner during our search for Eli.

Where we met the escapees, who risked death on their own terms rather than die making implements of war. Where I gave the woman Hannah the *sklaan*—the warmth-giving cloth—from K'lion's planet.

There, the slavery was about power. Who had it all, and who didn't have any.

Was I going to be taken to another rocket factory?

"Come on, little cocoa bean."

"I am *not* a 'little cocoa bean'!"

The man Howard was hauling me over to the horse-drawn wagon where the African woman sat. "Please be careful, Mr. Howard," Jefferson said. "Her Latin, after all, is better than yours."

Mr. Howard didn't think that was funny.

"I've got her now, Howard," the Nubian said. Was she some kind of visiting dignitary, to address the man so casually? "You go on back to making the world safe for the president."

She took my hand and pulled me up next to her.

"Afternoon, young lady. My name's Sally Hemings. What's yours?"

I want to see Eli. They took him off a wagon, but he didn't seem fully awake. I don't know where — or how — they found him, but he didn't appear well. Sally was summoned to help tend him. I want to follow, but some of the Centurions, the soldiers, are blocking my way to his tent.

So I remain in Sally's tent, where I have been left unguarded. I trust that the enhanced lingo-spot, the plasmechanical translation device I was given during my stay on K'lion's home world, will continue to record my experiences as a sort of living journal.

Yet I miss writing on my own scrolls. So much has changed and so quickly.

Including, apparently, the lingo-spots themselves. They are suddenly more *active*, more electric, as if they — like K'lion's ship — were taking on a life of their own.

At least, when I hear echoes coming from the lingo-spots that seem in no way connected to the conversation I am having, that is what I fear.

I hope I get to see Eli soon.

"Are you from Ethiopia?"

"What, young miss?"

"Are you an Ethiopian queen? On a royal visit?" I'd heard the one named Jefferson referred to as "president," a Roman-sounding title, which I assumed meant he presided over a lawmaking body, perhaps even a senate. It stood to reason, then, that this striking African woman, piloting her own wooden carriage, might also be a leader.

"Are you some kind of ruler? I want to understand what world I'm in."

"My Latin doesn't move that quickly," she said, straining to hear me. "Do you know French?"

French? It wasn't an Earth tongue I'd encountered, if this was indeed the same Earth. But she repeated the question in what I assume was that tongue, and parts of it were Latin-like.

"A queen?" I said again, still in Latin, more slowly, pointing to her.

There was a silence.

It was filled not with sound, but Mr. Howard's sharp looks. He didn't like the idea of my talking with Sally. Queen Sally.

When he turned away, I knew I was going to have to do something that allowed us to whisper, even with all the noise.

Show me.

Who said that?

I looked around. Only Sally and I were there.

But my lingo-spot was really tingling.

Show me.

This time I spun round so fast at the unseen voice that Sally jumped, jerking on the reins, causing the horses to rear up.

Show who? What?

Sally struggled to regain control of the horses.

"What are you trying to do, child?"

"I don't know," I admitted. Again using Latin. I was praying to find someone else connected to that voice. I didn't want to think that the lingo-spot could be acting . . . on its own.

Explaining any of this to Sally—or even myself—would have to wait.

"Thea," I said, tapping myself on the chest.

"Thea . . ." Sally repeated. "That's your name?"

I nodded.

"But you're . . . you're a runaway slave. Aren't you?"

"No." I shook my head. "Alexandria . . ." I tell her, sounding out the name of my home, hoping she will understand.

Her eyes widen in recognition. "That's close to where I live."

Then she *was* from Africa! A princess or a queen! I hoped I could make her understand.

She smiled in a sad way. "Yes, but we live in a different part of Virginia. In Monticello. I'm one of Mr. Jefferson's slaves. Though I expect he would prefer the word *servant.* Except there's not a whole lot of *choice* to it. On my part."

I had never heard of Virginia before. Sally also told me that Jefferson was the leader of his people, the Americans, who were also Eli's people, so perhaps we were close to his home and not near mine after all.

But why was there another Alexandria in this province of Virginia? What happened to the first one, *my* Alexandria, since the fire?

Sally didn't know about any fires, "except a small one in the kitchen last year." But she did tell me that Jefferson the president was currently far from Alexandria, or any place in Virginia, since he was traveling in secret with a team of adventurers led by two captains, named Lewis and Clark.

The captains and their men were off on a "great exploration," financed by Jefferson in order to find "secret routes to the ocean, and maybe look for giants."

Sally didn't think there really were giants, but Jefferson had developed a fascination with unearthing skeletal remains. He'd become obsessed with trying to understand the past, and therefore the future, by examining mysterious bones, both ancient and enormous, belonging to mysterious creatures. Creatures that seemed as unknowable as the gods — half animal, half human — that were worshiped back in Egypt.

Such bones were found here, where Jefferson's camp is made, near the great rivers Sally calls the Ohio and the Missouri. Jefferson's plan was to accompany Lewis and Clark to the Missouri in order to "say goodbye, and find more femurs," in Sally's words. "Mr. Jefferson says he's eager to learn the truth about America.

"Here's one truth." She looks over at me as she continues to guide the horses. We still have to raise our voices to hear each other, but Sally's not worried about Mr. Howard. "I have been Mr. Jefferson's friend for many years, and I know that he cares for me, too. But I am not able to leave his house as a free woman. As a plain American citizen. As a true friend. And now, you won't, either. I wonder what Mr. Lewis and Mr. Clark can find that will change the truth about that?"

"You there! Girl!"

I'm snapped out of my reverie. It's Mr. Howard, at the entrance to the tent.

"Sally wants you. She needs help."

Help. *Help for Eli?* I look around to see if there's anything I should gather up.

"No time for dawdling. The boy is getting worse."

I follow Mr. Howard outside.

I'm worried and scared, like I was for my mother. But when I think of Eli, there's another feeling, too. In my stomach.

One I've never had before.

One that makes me realize I really don't want to lose him.

Chapter Three

Eli: Incognitum

May 1804

I think I just talked with Thomas Jefferson. And I think Thea has been in to see me, too. But I was feverish when both things were happening, so I can't be sure.

And feverish or not, I don't know which is more surprising.

"What is happening in America that two young people show up out of nowhere, claiming to be lost, on such an otherwise pleasant afternoon?"

I'm pretty sure I heard Jefferson say that. He kind of likes to talk with extra words in his sentences.

"I won't let anything happen to you." That was Thea. She was dabbing cold rags on my head at the time.

As far as I could tell.

But even if it wasn't a dream, she's gone now, and there are guards outside the tent to keep me from leaving. I don't think I'm under arrest. I just don't think they know what to do with me yet.

And if I told them the truth—that I'm from the future, that I've been tangled up in time after an accident in my parents' lab, that I was whisked back to ancient Alexandria, where I met Thea, and that I bumped into Clyne, a talking dinosaur, while crossing the Fifth Dimension, time-traveled again to 1941, to World War II, to look for my mother, and then back to King Arthur's England to keep his sword Excalibur out of the hands of Nazis—if I told them all that, well, I don't know where they lock people up who they think are crazy or dangerous, but I bet they'd think there was something a little more wrong with me than just "fever."

I'm still not sure how we got here: Last thing I remember clearly is crossing the Fifth Dimension

again after saving Excalibur—all of us, Thea,
Clyne, and me—in the Saurian time-ship from
Clyne's planet. But our German prisoner, Rolf
Royd, the Dragon Jerk kid, managed to escape
when the ship itself started to . . . come *alive*
somehow. And in all the confusion, in the swirls
of color and time and possibility that move around
you when you time-travel, we were tossed directly
through the Fifth Dimension, like three Alices—
four, if I have to include Rolf—going down separate rabbit holes. And then we landed.

Here. Where they don't study American history in books, because they *are* American history, and where I don't think Alice and the rabbit
have even been written about yet. And you can
forget about the movie and game versions.

They don't even have baseball.

They don't even have Barnstormers! No Comnet games at all!

No wonder they had so much time to be historical and do famous stuff.

But wherever this is, whatever's going on, I
have to find Thea again, and then figure out if

Clyne is anywhere close by. Or any *when* close by, for that matter.

But it won't be easy. If Thomas Jefferson is president, that means I've landed way way back, even before Eisenhower and maybe both of the Roosevelts. Prehistory. When all the guys on stamps and money are still walking around, breathing air.

So far back, they don't even have *gasoline*-powered cars. And maybe not trains. I'll have to check.

But hey, that means there isn't any DARPA yet, either — no Defense Advanced Research Projects Agency. No Mr. Howe overseeing Dad's experiments, no military goons to keep watch over me, with their corny "Danger Boy" code name, and all their time-travel plans.

Which means the guys here shouldn't be too hard to duck: They won't have Night Vision goggles, or laser-guided stun guns, so I can start looking for Thea as soon as I crawl out the back of the tent.

Wait. Bayonets. They *do* have bayonets. They

have funny clothes and long coats, and bayonets on the ends of their rifles. And a couple of them just walked in. With the president.

"Taking leave of us, young squire?"

Jefferson spoke those words to my butt. My head was already poking out the back of the tent. Now I'm turned around, my arms are in the air, and those bayonets are looking pretty sharp.

Jefferson waves the soldiers away.

"I suspect I am not in too much jeopardy," the president tells them. "You may return to your posts outside. I will send out an alarum if the squire attempts another escape."

"What if he has another suspect hat, sir?"

Jefferson nods. "I intend to ask him about that. Now please leave us alone."

Jefferson looks for a place to sit, then pulls over a short barrel. He squints at some writing on the side. "Hmm. One of Captains Lewis and Clark's barrels of whiskey found its way into our supplies. I should return it. I suspect they will need all the spirits and Godspeed they can muster."

Jefferson sits down on top of the barrel and looks at me. He's big. Well, lanky and tallish.

Probably big enough to play basketball. At least, at this point in history. Everyone else seems pretty short. Do they even have basketball? Or do they just play soccer?

"Are you, in fact, an American?"

The question catches me off-guard. I'm not sure if it's supposed to be an insult, or what.

"Yes, sir, I am."

"Then might you know who I am?"

"Well, you're Thomas Jefferson. You were president."

He gives me a quizzical look. "I *am* president, young squire. Not that being president is necessarily the most desirable thing, mind. And since you know my name, who might you be?"

"Eli. Eli Sands."

"You seem very comfortable talking to a president, Master Sands."

"Sir, if I told you the reasons I'm not quite as shocked as I ought to be, you wouldn't believe me."

Jefferson cocks his head. I don't think my part of the conversation was going like he expected. "I am glad, young squire, that presidents can be trusted and regarded as equals. That is as it should be. But I prefer not to talk politics. Enough of that awaits me at home, when reelection time comes round. What brings you out west, young man?"

"Pardon me, Mr. President, sir."

"You may call me Mr. Jefferson."

"Mr. President Jefferson, sir. But I thought I heard we were somewhere around Missouri?"

"Yes."

"So we aren't in the West."

"How not?"

"The West is California, sir. Oregon. Washington. Utah. Arizona. Hollywood. Las Vegas. And my own home."

"Some of those names are Spanish territories. Some are Russian. Some I've never heard of— Hollywood? In any case, none of them is part of America. As yet." He shook his head. "And where is home for you, my strange young foundling?"

"In the Valley of the Moon. Near San Francisco. California."

"The moon, you say? And California, another name from a fairy tale, I believe." Jefferson pauses.

"That girl, that escaped slave, who helped heal you. She is known to you?"

"You mean Thea?"

"Her slave name appears to be Brassy. A runaway from New Orleans. Are you claiming she is yours?"

"Mine? *Mine?* My *slave?*" Now I am shocked, for completely different reasons, which maybe he still wouldn't believe. "You mean, because Thea's skin is a little darker than mine, you think—?"

Now it was my turn to cock my head. People say you can't know the future, but history always throws surprises at you, too. I was going to have to be careful: this was another tricky part of the past to be stuck in.

"Mr. President—"

"Jefferson."

"President Jefferson. I'm sorry. But that question kind of offends me."

Jefferson now stares at me as if I was some kind of Barnstormer character. He stands, finds an old cracked mug in the tent, kneels by the barrel, pops a big cork plug from near the top, tips the barrel, pours a little, pushes the cork back in, sets the barrel straight — then sits on it again.

He sips from the mug. "Normally, I prefer French wine. But such are the concessions of research in the field. I trust the good captains will not begrudge me a little of their grog. Besides," he adds, "I understand Sally and Brassy used some of this to minister to you and bring you round."

"They did?" I lick my lips and move my tongue, to see if there are any funny tastes in my mouth.

Jefferson is still trying to figure me out. "So then, young man, are you some kind of abolitionist? Did you help Brassy escape? Because I will tell you, as much as I'd hoped to leave politics behind for a while, anything to do with this slave business will put me in a delicate position. Even out here."

"It's really not so delicate, sir. Slavery is just plain wrong." Could I get arrested for talking to a president like that? "Can I see Thea?"

"I'm afraid, after what happened to my Treasury agent, Mr. Howard, that may not be possible."

"What happened to Mr. Howard?"

"He tried on your headdress, squire."

"You mean my Seals cap?" Oh, no. That will scramble the time-charge of this Howard guy's protons. I hope he hasn't vanished. Or gone crazy.

"It seems to cause a kind of fever in the wearer. If it spreads, you may yet cause the president himself to be quarantined." After another sip, Jefferson leans over. "Master Sands, you are clearly a young man of great means and wiles. But you may have to be remanded to United States custody until we understand the nature of your being here.

"You see, even putting the matter of slaves aside, my sending of Captains Lewis and Clark and their Corps of Discovery on a journey west is itself a finely tuned political matter, and I must orchestrate it well. My goal is to have them explore the areas of my Louisiana Purchase, a fine expanse of territory I have just bought from the emperor Napoleon, to record scientific curiosities throughout the far west, and most importantly, to discover a direct water route to the Pacific. The American experiment is expanding toward those shores."

"Yes, sir."

"Many in Congress expect this expedition to

fail. They expect the Corps to fall prey to bands of hostile Indians, or fierce giants, or other creatures that may roam out there. They think I am ridiculous to fund this expedition."

He rubs his forehead and sips his whiskey, then makes a face. "I really should have brought more wine from home. This is much too rough. But it will serve." He lowers the mug. "The atmosphere in Washington is so rancid now that I decided to slip out of town myself, *incognitum,* as it were, accompanying the Corps nearly as far as St. Louis, their true launching point, in order to pursue a small hobby."

"What hobby is that, sir?" I try to concentrate on Jefferson, but being kept from Thea makes me edgy, plus there's suddenly a lot of shouting outside—both the human and the horse kind.

"Bones, Master Sands. Bones." He turns toward the tent flap. "What is that contemptible racket? Are there no quiet mornings to be had anywhere in this country?"

The morning gets even less quiet. Mr. Howard barges into the tent. He's bathed in sweat, and his eyes are bulging.

"Terrible lizards, sir!"

"Shouldn't you be getting medical attention, Mr. Howard?" Jefferson asks.

The cap may not have made him disappear, but it's sure affected him.

"Sir, I cannot rest when we have information on just how dangerous the future of this expedition—and therefore your electoral future as president—might be!"

"What information is that?"

"I repeat: 'Terrible lizards, sir!'"

Jefferson sighs. "Which lizards, Mr. Howard?"

"A French fur trapper has just wandered into camp! His name is Banglees. He spent last winter in the Dakotas with the Mandan Indians and the Hidatsas! Said they were telling stories about a big terrible lizard in the wild who walks like a man and talks! He said he tried to track the lizard down, but an awful snowstorm came up and he almost froze. He says now the lizard may have saved him. Claims it was some kind of creature asking him for an *orange,* and when he came to, he was back with the Indians."

Jefferson shakes his head. "Has this Banglees

been wearing young Master Sand's fever hat, perchance?"

"Sir!" This Howard guy says nearly every word like he's warning people about a fire. "We may have to cancel the expedition! We may have to arm them with cannons!"

"Perhaps you should return to bed rest, Mr. Howard. And perhaps I should attend to this . . . Banglees." Jefferson rises to his feet, sets the mug down, and manages to smile at me, a little. "Perhaps, Master Sands, I am not as far from the president's office as I had hoped. We shall resume later."

But it was hard for me to pay much attention to President Jefferson right then. I was figuring out how I could talk to this French fur-trapper guy myself.

To find out more about a lizard who asks for oranges.

Clyne.

Clyne is out there somewhere. He's been discovered. And he's in danger.

Chapter Four

Clyne: Arrak-du

This may be my last homework report for two reasons, both of which accelerate my head-spindles and give me brain transgressions.

The first of the reasons is this: The plasmechanical material from my home world of Saurius Prime, the breakthrough substance that makes so much Saurian technology possible, appears to be infected with slow pox.

I grant that this is a conclusion based on field research, using radically imperfect equipment and *gerk-skizzy* methods.

Or perhaps *gerk-skizzy* is too unkind. But I have had to rely on an old science project trick from Third Step Elemental School.

"Imagine you are in the *arrak-du,*" our teachers would tell us, "the lost lands, and you must confirm the essential nature of a new specimen you have found. How would you proceed?"

One of the solutions to that problem is to fashion a basic microscope lens out of a sheet of ice. It takes much patience and long sitting and adept use of one's claws. Due to the distortions that come with slight ice melt, I have made three of them over the last pair of days, in order to confirm my results.

I was prompted to do this for several reasons, among them: the anomalous behavior of the Saurian time-vessel, which resulted in abrupt ejection of my friends and me from the Fifth Dimension; my return to Earth Orange, human year sometime in their nineteenth century, but with no trace of my human companions nearby; strange interjections from the lingo-spots, which are suddenly operating on broader frequencies and seem to want to participate in—and not merely translate—conversations; and the fact that I am surrounded by vast tracts of snow and ice and have little else to do at the moment but work on possible extra credit.

In fact, I may just fashion a fourth ice lens and take another small sample of the lingo-spot material from behind my ear, to confirm these results once more.

I have been consulting the *National Weekly Truth*, one of the journals of news and logical deduction distributed in Eli's time. I have kept a crumpled copy in my chrono-suit, the one with the heading LIZARD MAN IN THE WOODS!, with an artist's rendering that follows, saved as an additional piece of evidence that my time here on Earth Orange was real and not the fevered imaginings of someone off in an interdimensional *arrak-du* of his own.

Though I wonder if now I've ended up in a mammal *arrak-du:* of the few humans I've encountered here, none seems to have heard of oranges.

Meanwhile, the *Weekly Truth* provides some helpful medical background:

FIVE THINGS THE GOVERNMENT
DOESN'T WANT YOU TO KNOW
ABOUT SLOW POX!

1. This isn't the "slow pox" of the Middle Ages—famously seen during the outbreak in Alexandria around the year 400. This is a mutant strain that escaped from a government lab!

2. There is no cure—but if you survive, you're immune. Remember: this new form of slow pox attacks not just the blood but brain function, too. You might wind up a zombie subject to outside control!

3. Aliens don't catch slow pox! Could the sudden reappearance of the disease be the first attack in an imminent invasion from outer space? Is our government helping aliens turn taxpayers into zombies?

4. The effects of slow pox work . . . slowly! But the disease is still spreading, despite what you hear from less reliable news sources!

5. Government detention centers are coming soon! Slow pox will be the excuse! Will *you* be the victim? Not if you read the *National Weekly Truth* and stay informed!

This is my theory: Part of what makes plasmechanics a "smart" technology is the material's ability to adapt and change according to prevailing conditions. Not just through computation, but by incorporating biology. That's how the lingo-spot is able to interact with the vibrations and synapse-firings of the wearer in order to translate.

From what I know, slow pox acts on mammal blood and brains: it causes much lobe confusion. It mimics the cellular reproduction of nerve endings and makes a false version of the nerve tissue, which reroutes and distorts the signals. This often leads to paralysis. Similarly, in the bloodstream, real cells are poorly replicated, so the blood itself becomes a kind of wasteland, unable to clean itself or run freely through vein systems.

A bad set of conditions, biologically speaking. It makes Searing Scale Syndrome seem like a picnic, in contrast.

In fact, I initially thought slow pox had infected that mammal Banglees, when I came across him out here in these ice fields.

Instead, he was almost frozen. Coldflummoxed, by letting his campfire die down while he dozed.

After I helped respark the flames and thaw him out, he blinked at me several times.

"Eh — you mean, I am not dead?" he asked.

"Evidently not," I told him.

"Then how is it you are here, *mon ami*, if I am not? Are you not from Heaven, or the other place?"

I wondered if "Heaven, or the other place" referred to some kind of *arrak-du.*

"I have taken some very engaging missteps in space and time," I told him, "which have all construed to bring me here."

"You mean you are lost?"

"I am doing extended field research."

"Ah, well. If zat means you are lizard people, I suppose it ees my job to kill you and take your skin and skull with me."

"Your entire employment is based on a graphic recipe for harming me?"

"I am a trapper."

He tightened the mammal furs — borrowed permanently, it appeared, from other mammals —

more tightly around himself and moved closer to the flames.

"But I am also cold, and I have been out a long time, so I am tired. And while I am not convinced *complètement* zat I am alive or zat you are real, I will spend the next hours until sunup talking to you, if for no other reason than to make sure I stay awake."

"Then we will talk of—"

Nika-tc.

The word came out of my mouth before I knew what I was saying. "Home." Saurian for "home."

But it didn't feel like I was the one saying it.

It felt like the lingo-spot.

Though I've never known a lingo-spot to use Saurian before.

"You will have to make more sense than zat, *mon ami,* whether you are imaginary or not."

Banglees and I talked of many things, including the stories of the lizard people. Once he thawed, he seemed much nimbly again with the kind of *zrk-kttl* energy I have come to expect of mammals, and in the morning, he was on his way.

I believe I have met the lizard people, and

they are me. I wonder, though, if there are others?

Since then, the lingo-spot has still occasionally whispered to me of *arrak-du* and *nika-tc.*

And looking through the slightly distorted ice lens I have fashioned to recheck my results, I think the slow pox has affected the cellular structure of the plasmechanical substance by allowing a mutation that the microtechnology then tries to "fix."

Which is to say, slow pox virus caused pretend nerve cells to form based on the slightest electrical impulses between cells. The engineered micromachines then "repaired" this suddenly growing tissue. And somehow made it work.

The slow pox mutation is, in this instance, allowing a nervous system to form.

And therefore, allowing the plasmechanical tissue to function at an even higher level of intelligence.

That might explain what happened to the Saurian time-vessel.

But this is all untested theory, and there is little equipment here to verify results, until I get home.

Nika-tc.

If I get home.

Can lost lands become home if one is stranded in them long enough?

Which brings up another question: If the plas-mechanical tissue was fabricated on Saurius Prime, how could slow pox affect the Saurian biology?

Slow pox affects mammals.

The only mammals we have there are small—and scurrying. Are we using them for science in ways I am unaware of, or has the slow pox virus mutated already?

Because of a previous exposure to Saurians?

"Many Lights?"

I turn, *gerk-skizzy* myself, caught by surprise.

I didn't hear my friend approach.

Like the other humans I have seen up here, he is bundled up in the borrowed skins of other mammals. But unlike the other humans, he is the only one I now call friend: North Wind Comes.

"Many Lights—they are hunting you now."

He calls me Many Lights. I have learned his tongue. I have also, alas, given him some of my lingo-spot, for better understanding.

I now must hope that I haven't given my friend slow pox as well.

Which brings me to the second reason this may be my last homework assignment: If the plasmechanical material itself is infected, there may be no way back to Saurius Prime.

"They are hunting you now, Many Lights, and I believe they mean to kill you."

However, staying may not be so easy, either.

Chapter Five

Eli: Upriver

I'm in St. Louis, it's raining, and I'm being sent to a pirogue.

"The boy *should* be with the dugout crew! Let him row!"

"Put him with the keelboat and he can help us *push* our way upriver!"

Now I just have to figure out what a pirogue *is*. The keelboat, though, you can't miss: it looks like a barge, made of big wooden blocks—kinda squared off, right down to the cabinets plopped down one end. Least, I think they're cabinets—all the men from Lewis and Clark's Corps of Discovery are stuffing things into them.

Woof! Rrraawwfff!

And Seaman, Lewis's big black shaggy Newfoundland dog, is smelling as many of the supplies as he can. That is, when he's not adding his own: sometimes he shows up with a couple squirrels in his mouth, which the men then fry up to eat.

Yuck. I wonder if there's some real food.

"Try the pirogue, lad. The red one. You can help me row."

I look up and recognize the grinning man in the wet, smelly leather. He seems to have a lot more whiskers on his face than last time, though it's only been a day or two since I've seen him.

"Charles Floyd," he says, sticking out his hand. "I'm one of the sergeants. But you can just call me Kentuck. That's a nickname."

I shake his hand. Although his skin is wet, I can feel the hard blisters on it. The shake is friendly. "You ain't from Kentucky, too, by any chance?"

I can see, behind the whiskers and the grime

on his face, that he's actually kinda young. I mean, he's older than me—he's not a kid—but he's one of those young grownups, the kind who don't have kids of their own yet, or who are still in college, or in a band, or in a comedy show on one of the vidnets.

"No, I'm from—" I stop. I better not keep saying "Valley of the Moon," or they won't let me go on this expedition at all.

Lewis and Clark's expedition.

Woof!

I'm going with Lewis and Clark.

Rrwwooof!

"I'm from New Jersey."

"Well met, then. *I* am from Pennsylvania."

I turn, and there's another young grownup, but with clothes a little fancier than Floyd's—even though they're getting wet, like everyone else's—and a clean-shaven face.

"Patrick Gass, at your service."

"Gassy's gonna write about us. He's keepin' a journal," Floyd says. "Told him I was gonna keep one, too. Just to spite him."

Rrrraawwf!

Seaman's jumping around near Floyd, clearly excited about something. Maybe there's some leftover squirrel meat?

" 'Scuse me a minute," Floyd says. "Even in the rain, he wants to play." He takes a really scruffy round—well, *sort* of round—leather ball from somewhere inside his jacket, and throws it for Seaman, who scampers off and goes sniffing for it in the mud by the riverbank.

Gass takes out a thick, compact leather book with heavy paper bound in the middle. "Many of us are keeping journals, including Captain Lewis. The difference between mine and Kentuck's is that mine will actually be readable." He stuffs the journal back into his coat, to keep it as dry as possible.

I guess there's no point telling them to wait a couple hundred years, then they won't have to write at all—they can just talk out loud and have their thoughts recorded by a combination of digits and liquid memory chips.

"So are you joining us in the pirogue?"

"Well, sure." I look from Floyd—Kentuck—back to Gassy. "Which one's the pirogue?"

Floyd points. It's one of the canoes.

At least, they're canoe-*shaped*. But each one seems to be dug out of a single tree trunk. Like some kind of project in wood shop that got way out of control.

"Don't let him ride in there if he's going to fall out! The president says to be careful!"

It's Mr. Howard. Even with the rain, you can still tell he's sweaty—you can see the difference between what he's putting out and what the clouds are dropping.

"Yes, sir," Floyd agrees with a smile.

Seaman scampers back up, drops the ball from his mouth, then shakes out his fur, spraying us all with more water.

Mr. Howard looks completely unamused.

"The boy is to return in the spring, with the artifacts you send back downriver. He is to come back with the lizard man!"

"*Yes,* sir." Floyd nods. A kind of nod where you can tell he doesn't really think there is a "lizard man."

"And you!" Howard has turned away and found Lewis and dragged him away from a conversation he was having with Clark and York. "The president says you are to keep special watch over this boy! You, and not your men!"

Wiping his face, he adds, "And mind that dog of yours, too."

Lewis doesn't wipe his face at all, letting the water run down his nose and over his mouth as he speaks. "Mr. Howard. May I remind you that my orders are to explore a continent, not act as nursemaid to some runaway squire."

"His safety is in your hands!"

"Yes, well, given the high odds against the entire party returning in one piece, you may want to consider other hands. Mine are full. Though the boy is welcome." Lewis looks at me, and through the gray dampness, I can see that he's almost smiling. Which for him is like breaking into a full grin. "After all, if the boy is an omen or portent of some sort, we might as well have him working for us instead of against us. Assure the president that he will be every bit as safe as any member of the Corps of Discovery."

Rrrrooowf!

"Including Seaman."

This answer doesn't quite satisfy Mr. Howard, and he turns to make a beeline for Clark, who sees him coming and, along with York, suddenly gets busy loading more crates into the keelboats.

It's Jefferson's fault—from Mr. Howard's perspective—that I am here, being sent along with the Corps. Or at least it can be blamed on Jefferson's permission.

I took a chance with him during our conversation in the tent. He seemed pretty reasonable, for a president. "I know who that terrible, orange-eating lizard is," I said after Mr. Howard brought him the news from Banglees, the fur trapper. My voice was only a little shaky.

"How? Have you met him? Tracked him, perhaps? Are you in fact a young fur trapper, then, come down from Canada? Perhaps that is why you referred to your hat as a 'Seals' cap."

"I have . . . journeyed with him. The lizard."

"In the unexplored lands? So the stories are true? These bones we're finding, the bones of giant creatures—huge elephants and tigers. They still live? In the wilds? I knew my studies of them would not be in vain!" Jefferson was getting excited and began pacing. "I believe many kinds of giants once lived in America, and many more may yet roam the West!" He spun and faced me. "Are you a Welsh Indian?"

"A what? Sir?"

Turned out he was referring to a legend about a tribe of "white Indians" that were supposed to be descended from some Welsh prince, or something, though no one's ever seen them. But I guess a lot of people back then believed funny things. They didn't have the Comnet — not even radio or TV — to help them figure things out.

"I'm not a Welsh Indian, Mr. President," I told him. "But the lizard and I do come from . . . a distant land."

"Earlier, you talked about the moon."

"Closer than the moon, sir." I decided not to complicate things by telling him about Saurius Prime or the Fifth Dimension. "We came in a ship."

"Then you *have* discovered a northwest passage? A direct water route to the Pacific from the inland rivers?"

"It was a different kind of ship, sir. It doesn't go on water."

"A land ship, then? May I see it?"

"Well, we've lost it." That was when I saw my opening. "But the lizard man may know where to find it. That is, if he's not harmed."

"I will give them the sternest instructions, Master Sands, to bring this creature back alive."

"But he knows me, Mr. Jefferson. He trusts me."

"But I cannot let you go. Aside from possibly being an abolitionist, you are somewhat of a specimen yourself."

"But, sir, I believe I offer the best hope of actually bringing the lizard man back alive. Imagine the scientific bonanza if you could talk to him yourself."

Jefferson looked at me with surprise and suspicion. He shook his head, looked at the whiskey in his hand, and set it down. "No, I really must stick with French wine. My time in Paris spoiled me." Then he turned back to me. "Perhaps that seal-fur hat of yours has addled your brains, as well. Even if this lizard *talks,* as the French trapper, and now you, claim, and even if I let you go—how do I know you'll return and not try to escape with him? Or harm the expedition?"

"That's simple." I decided to take another chance. "I'm coming back for . . . Brassy. But you have to protect her. You can't turn her in."

That was all I could do to help Thea right then. I hoped it was enough.

Now the look on the president's face was only surprise. "I suppose I can let her join my household staff. Sally will see to her." He looked at me, sighed, then nodded. "I will have Mr. Howe ride with you into St. Louis and remand you to the care of Captains Clark and Lewis. I will instruct them to send you back downriver next spring, after you reach the Mandan people."

"Can I see Brassy, sir? Before I go?"

"Impossible. She's with Sally, and were you to visit her so openly, we'd just stir the pot and get everyone upset. I shall keep her safe at Monticello until you return. We can then work out the riddle of this escaped slave. Meanwhile, see that you return, Master Sands. I could use a bona fide scientific discovery to justify all this expense to Congress."

President Jefferson offered his hand. "Welcome to America, lad."

"Biscuit barrel!" The words are screamed at me, and I barely have time to get out of the way before the rolling barrel would have knocked me into the river. It still catches my leg with a sharp thump and sends me sprawling on the wet pier.

The rain is coming down much harder now.

There are a whole bunch of us going — I've counted forty in all. Plus Seaman. And I don't know how they plan to feed us: I've seen those "biscuits" and they're like hard, flat, stale crackers — pre-stale, really, so they can't get in any worse shape during a long journey. Besides the biscuits, they're also taking molasses, flour, a bunch of dried meat, whiskey, and brandy. No juice boxes, no rice milk, no boxes of cereal — nothing for me.

Maybe I'll be able to pick apples along the way.

There's also something Lewis calls "portable

soup," which is kind of thick and oozy and looks like it might belong in a tar pit. I wonder if Lewis was in one of his gloomy moods when he made it.

As for drinking water, I guess the plan is to actually drink the river water during the voyage. It's kind of amazing that there was ever a time you could just drink straight from a river. I bet Lewis would get even gloomier if I told him about all the pollution that was coming in the future.

There are also lots of guns — the long, *Nutcrackery* old-fashioned ones. No beam or particle weapons of any kind. These are gunpowder guns, where you have to stuff the barrel with shot and powder and can get off only one blast at a time.

I wonder if people feel safer in this period, when even the deadliest weapons move so slowly?

I bet a lot of animals won't feel so safe, though, and I'm not talking about Seaman's squirrels. Part of the food plan, I'm pretty sure, is to do some hunting along the way. I'm guessing there won't be any veggie burgers.

"Let me help you with that." I turn, and it's York. He's the only black man on the whole expedition. He's supposed to be Clark's "slave,"

but to look at someone and have to think that—
to have to attach that word to them—makes me
feel small.

"Bringin' lots of stuff, ain't they?" York asks,
as he offers me a hand. I hold on—nearly slipping
out of his grasp—and manage to get back on my
feet. My leg is still sore, but I don't let on as I
move to help him with the barrel.

"Is it all just food?" I ask. "What are they
going to explore with?"

"They got the usual stuff. Guns. Some tools to
fix things. Compasses to figure out where we're
goin' and where we just been. Books to write
stuff down in. And lots of things to trade with the
Indians. Look."

York shows me a small gold coin with Thomas
Jefferson's head on it. "This is supposed to be a
peace offerin', to let 'em know who the big white
chief in Washington is."

"Why would they care about that?" I ask.
"Don't they have their own chiefs?"

York laughs. "I guess we all get chiefs we don't
necessarily choose."

We set the barrel in the keelboat, then go to

lift another of the wooden crates. I want to keep talking, in order to take my mind off how cold and damp I am.

"What are you bringing, Mr. York?"

"Aw, you ain't really ought to call me Mister. I am bringin' my own rifle, though, which we ain't supposed to have as slaves. But out here, Mr. Clark allows it. Mostly, I'm just glad to be goin' someplace where nobody will know who's a slave and who ain't."

"York, you're talkin' that young fella's ear off, and he's liable to melt clean away afore your eyes in this rain!"

"Kentuck!"

It's Floyd, with a big grin on his face, holding up a buckskin jacket and one of those wide floppy hats. "You'll need these to keep dry."

"Dry" is more of an idea than an actual possibility at this point, since the jacket and hat are dripping water. But I take them, and put them on. Besides blending in better, I am a lot warmer.

And I probably look like Huck Finn or Tom Sawyer.

"So which of you layabouts is ready to get going?"

I turn to see Clark, standing up in a pirogue. He smiles, too, like Kentuck, but more with his eyes. Maybe that's why Jefferson matched him up with Lewis—like being a team manager in Barnstormers and picking a lineup—they each have opposite strengths, like the moon and the sun: One keeps things in shadows, so you can't tell how they'll turn out, the other warms you up and tells you everything will be all right.

"I'm with you, sir!" Floyd says.

"You actually askin' me for an opinion, Mr. Clark?" York means it as a joke, but it runs a little deeper than that.

"I'm actually telling you men that someone else will beat us to the Pacific unless we get going!" Clark means it as a joke, too, but it also helps him avoid an answer.

Floyd and York and I load the last of the crates into the keelboat. I look around through the gray sleet and notice we're the last three men on the docks.

York helps me into the square boat. The man paddling Clark's pirogue pulls it alongside.

"Ride with me, Master Sands," Clark says. "It would be my privilege."

I look around. I'm not sure what I'm waiting for, maybe someone to nod that it's okay, as I try to step carefully from the keelboat—which is still tied up to the dock—into the dugout canoe. I slip on the wet wood again and fall in, landing by Clark's boots and banging my head.

"You *must* be careful with that boy!"

It's Howard. He's reemerged from the mist and stands there, the same mixture of sweat and rain covering his body. He should be shivering. He should be really cold. But it just looks like he's on fire.

"You must keep him alive!"

Howard is pointing and hopping around on the small dock. He's going to fall in the river if he's not careful.

"Are you all right?" Clark asks.

I rub my forehead. There's a bump already forming. But I'll be okay.

"I think so. I've had worse." I don't want to get left behind now.

"Welcome to the Corps of Discovery." Clark has his hand out and I take it.

The keelboat with York, Floyd, and Lewis has shoved off, and the oarsmen in our pirogue begin paddling, taking us into the river.

We're moving.

"Remember! The president has ordered you to come back alive!" Howard is shouting as we leave, like he can change the will of the universe all by himself.

Meanwhile, I'm rubbing my head and trying to remember enough of my history to know whether any of us actually make it back — or not.

Rrrooowwwf.

Chapter Six

Thea: East

May 1804

"He won't beat you. He won't whip you. I'll tell him to keep you in the house with me. He's tolerable, for a master. He even took me to Paris once."

"Paris? Is where?"

Sally and I are shouting out words to each other because we are riding on top of the carriage taking Mr. Thomas President Jefferson back to his palace. Or wherever it is he dwells. He calls it Monticello.

Perhaps I should refer to him as Mr. Jefferson President, instead. I am still not sure of the correct way to arrange the title, though I know this does seem to be an early form of the same govern-ment Eli lived under, much like the Romans had during their republic phase.

Jefferson is a leader here, a kind of regent—and a man of import. Sally is his slave. And now, apparently, I am, too. Or rather, I am in his cus-tody until I can be "returned." Where? To whom?

And how much farther from Eli will I be taken?

I helped minister to him when he was still gripped by fever. Perhaps our displacement in time has a cumulative effect, becoming harder and harder on us each time.

I wasn't able to question Eli when his fever broke. I was already back in the slave tent. And then Eli was gone, dispatched on some kind of mission by this same Jefferson President.

History and chance are ever interfering with a growing friendship.

At the moment, the peculiarities of this juncture in history—everyone's reaction to skin pigment and heritage—force me to be counted a slave. And so I must remain until I can plan an escape.

According to Sally, she is lent a certain dignity

not given to others forced into servitude. Jefferson even invited her to ride inside the wagon with him, but she declined, preferring to stay outside, on the bench, with Mr. Howard. She makes him uncomfortable. Occasionally she even takes the reins of the horses from him, holding them like she did when I first laid eyes on her.

"Paris?" I repeat. I am still wearing K'lion's lingo-spot. Indeed, it seems to be changing into a permanent feature of my physiology. I still rely on it here, in spite of my worries that when I hear a word a split second before it's spoken or thought of, the lingo-spot may be exerting a mind of its own.

But I have yet to fully master the "English" that Sally, Jefferson President, Eli, and all the others use, though I have picked up a few words and phrases.

Until I can give some of the lingo-spot to Sally, those few words are all I have to communicate with. Aside from whatever Latin Sally remembers. Between the two tongues, we cobble together more conversation.

"Yes, dear. Paris. In France. That's not where you're from, is it?"

"Alexandria," I tell her again, practicing English. "No slave." I hope she understands.

"You poor lost thing. How can you be from a town in Virginia and not be a slave? Maybe you are Brassy, and you've just lost your mind." She lowers her voice so that Mr. Howard, who is studiously pretending to ignore us, will definitely not be able to hear. "They'll eventually have to return you to New Orleans, you know."

I have to let her know I can't go to New Orleans, either. I have to let her know who I really am. In order to fully explain everything. Perhaps, if I take advantage of the carriage bumps, I can dab some lingo-spot on her and make it look "accidental."

"We'll have to teach you better English," Sally says. "Jefferson will help. Wants his slaves to be educated. He discusses science and philosophy with me all the time, tells me how he still misses Martha, his late wife. He talks to me just like a free person. Yet he turns around and says it wouldn't be fair to let his own slaves go. Says we been raised like children and couldn't make our way in the world." She shakes her head. "This coming from the same man who tried to put a passage about ending slavery into the Declaration of Independence, till they made him take it out. I think slavery's got white people all mixed up inside. I think, really, it's worse on the spirits of the people who own the slaves, compared to the people who are the slaves. Some of them, anyway."

She doesn't keep her voice low for that last observation. I wonder if Jefferson President could hear her, too, inside the carriage.

"Martha died almost twenty years ago . . . and I've lived at Monticello, or traveled with that man, ever since. But he still won't let me call him Thomas. He says we can't be friends in public. But I won't call him Mister, either, and certainly not Master, if he's going to be that way. So I just call him Jefferson."

Then Sally closes her eyes and leans into the rushing air. She looks serene. "So many mysteries. Starting with people's hearts."

Show me.

That voice again.

Show me.

It's not Sally who's talking. . . .

Show me!

It's the lingo-spot.

The lingo-spot is exerting a will of its own now. Asking, or letting the thought be known, that it wants to be shown—given—to someone else. The way Eli gave some to me, back in Alexandria. The way I did, at Peenemünde, with the escaping prisoners.

Shared.

I reach behind my ear, feeling the spongy area where the lingo-spot melds into my skin. What does it want? To help us? And why is the organic/mechanical mass that makes up the lingo-spot suddenly exerting a will of its own, the way K'lion's time-vessel did? What is happening to the Saurian technology?

I look at my fingertips and touch the pulsing, glistening ointment there.

Maybe . . . ?

I look at it again.

Maybe it wants to spread because it wants to *reproduce*?

For reasons I can't explain, I feel my cheeks flushing.

But yes . . . reproduce, spread like a . . .

"Fever?"

It's Sally, leaning over, almost off-balance, touching my face. "You're turning all red, child."

Mr. Howard doesn't like her moving around. "You crazy girl! Sit down, now!"

I'm no child, but Sally's a grown woman. Why does he call her "girl"?

She looks at Mr. Howard, then stands up a little higher. "We all burn with fever! We burn with the life force of the universe! It surrounds us all and *lifts* us!"

"Sit *down!*" Mr. Howard isn't watching the road at all.

Sally stands even taller, spreading her arms against the wind. "*No one* is a slave!" She's yelling into the wind. Then she turns to me. "Not in their souls."

"Now!"

We hit some holes and ruts. One of the horses stumbles.

Mr. Howard jerks the reins in reaction — too late.

Sally's thrown forward. Without thinking, I reach out, grabbing just enough of her garment to break her fall. She twists and clutches the seat railing as Mr. Howard struggles to regain control of the horses before we spill over.

But I spill over, anyway, from catching Sally. And there is nobody to catch me. I hear screams.

What a silly death, so far from home, before I was able even to . . .

Reproduce.

My face flushes again. I will die with crimson cheeks . . .

"Brassy!"

. . . trampled by . . .

OOOF!

. . . the horses — I'm tangled up with the horses, the still-moving horses . . .

"Sooysaa! Sooysaa! Sooysaa!"

I scream out the word for "horse" that groomers and trainers in the palace stables used in Alexandria.

Holding on to the straps around one horse's neck, I pull myself up—"*Sooysaa!*"—on the running animal's back.

Everything is still a blur. I grip the horse, trying to hold on.

Without realizing it, I press the lingo-spot substance into the base of the horse's skull. "Sooysaa . . ." I repeat, over and over.

The first horse slows as I keep talking, and as its panic recedes, the other horse follows, until finally, at last, the carriage is brought to a stop.

"Sooysaa . . ." I stroke its neck, still clutching. "Thank you."

The horse's eyes bulge. For a moment, I think it might bolt again.

And then I realize . . . the lingo-spot. The *lingo-spot.* I've put the lingo-spot on the horse.

Show me.

Maybe the horse understands—and in understanding, has grown terrified.

"Brassy."

It's a male voice. But the name's not mine.

"Are you all right?"

I stroke the horse's mane. I won't answer to a slave name.

"Brassy!"

There's more dignity in talking to a horse.

Chapter Seven

Clyne: North Wind Comes

Snow is falling again, covering up the ice lenses I made and, with them, any hope of continuing my research here in the field. A warm lab would be nice. But until I find one, I content myself with eating a new food, which comes, once again, in surprising colors, while taking in the news that I have been mistaken for a mystical being and that my life is in jeopardy.

It is another bracing day here on Earth Orange.

The new food is called maize. I believe it is the forebear of the grain known as corn, which I read about in some discarded nutritional guides—cookbooks—that I encountered while foraging for sustenance in Eli's time. That was when I was an "outlaw," and the security forces in his world were looking for me. I seem to be back in Eli's world once again, though in a time before policing was so widespread.

"Look. In the distance there. Coming toward us." I point for the benefit of my friend, whose eyesight is, after all, only mammalian. "Two buffalo."

"Yes. We should leave before they get here," he tells me. "Buffalo leave tracks. The hunters who are coming for you could follow those tracks. We should take you back to your den. You need to stay hidden."

"You said this place would keep them away. This Spirit Mound. I like to come here because it's so quiet. It brings such a slowdown of body flow and thought. I was able to focus on some modest field research."

I need to share my results with him, but my friend is in a hurry. "The tales of the Spirit Mound won't keep Crow's Eye away. He thinks you may be one of the spirits. Grown to incredible size. Which would only bring him that much more glory as a warrior were he to kill you."

"Snow falls little on Saurius Prime. I have never seen so much territory chill-factored and freeze-blanketed all at once. I have created ice lenses for only the second time in my life! Can't we wait for the buffalo? After all, they may wish to deliver greetings to their cousin, who you have wrapped around your shoulders."

The young shaman called North Wind Comes pulls the mammal fur more tightly around his body. "Just my luck. I train to be a shaman to bring wisdom to my people. Instead, I find a serpent being, a totem more suited to a desert people than to Mandans, who makes comments about my ability to stay alive in bone-chilling weather. I can see that I am not meant to come by wisdom very easily." He looks at me. "How is a desert lizard like you staying warm?"

"I am a little frost-strewn. But the standard chrono-suit I wear resists weather excess. For a while." I would smile at my friend, but I have discovered that Saurian mouths often contain more teeth than human mammals are comfortable with. Plus, the teeth have corn stuck in them, and my tongue keeps trying to flick the pieces out. "I am not trying to offend you, North Wind."

"No. I suspect not. But why must I work so hard at convincing you to preserve your own life, Many Lights? Crow's Eye is the warrior who vowed to find you and bring you in, and he is not interested in your tales of seasonal displacement."

Seasonal displacement is the phrase North Wind Comes uses for "time travel." His people, his tribe, the Mandans, who live in this place they call the Dakotas, don't have quite the same words for "temporal" or "time" that Eli's people do. They don't think of time as a straight line, a one-way river. They think of it, somewhat correctly, as a circle. And they don't have many words for it, because they don't monitor their lives minute by minute, as is common in Eli's day. In North Wind's time, they tend to think of seasons.

"Why does this Crow's Eye warrior want me? Are his people afraid of me, too?"

"The warriors imagine killing you will make them brave."

The security forces in Eli's time captured me, and I found myself in the custody of two medium-high-ranking mammals, a Mr. Howe and a woman named Thirty. They played strange word games with me, believing I possessed mysterious "information" about a possible planetary invasion.

Perhaps they thought I was from the Spirit Mound, too.

I was then rescued by my friend Thea, who was piloting a time-vessel from my home world, and we reunited with Eli, who was in the company of a king named Arthur. Eli was trying to convince him to give up his sword.

There was also another mammal, named Rolf Royd, from someplace called the Reich, who had rather sad and frightening beliefs, and he wanted the sword, too. Eventually the king decided to keep it—which I was led to believe made for a surprising twist on recorded mammal history—and the four of us headed into the Fifth Dimension. When the plasmechanical material that made up the time-craft became more animated, pitching us out straight into the flow of time, once again, the three of us — Eli, Thea, and I — were separated.

But even infected plasmechanical material wouldn't explain why we were brought to this particular time. Usually when there's a disruption in the time stream, the attraction is a type of "prime nexus" — a moment when something happens, however large or small, that changes everything that comes after.

What is the nexus here?

If the buffalo know, they aren't saying.

Indeed, they aren't even moving now. They've stopped to raise their heads. Since they come equipped with heavy coats, perhaps they are enjoying the freeze-blanketing, too.

"Uh-oh." North Wind worries a lot.

Being tossed out of the time-craft felt like an *uh-oh,* too, for a few short beats of time. Everything was a blur of overwhelming feeling. That was soon replaced by the blur of almost infinite *possibility,* a mix of swirling colors that resolved, finally, into night air and stars. That was when I found myself staring into the eyes of the young mammal who speaks to me now: North Wind Comes.

He was the first human to discover me here. Or perhaps I discovered him. He says he was undergoing a coming-of-age ritual, called a vision quest, when we met. "Just my luck," he said, after we talked a while. "I have a vision who's stranded and needs to be fed." It may have been what the humans call a joke.

North Wind jokes about his luck a lot.

I stayed outdoors with him then—his "quest" was like the bush walks we had as growing nestlings on Saurius Prime—and we talked and shared our stories.

North Wind is slightly older than Eli and Thea, and he comes from a specific nest-community, called a tribe. His people call themselves Mandans, and they live close to another tribe, the Hidatsas, to whom the young warrior Crow's Eye belongs. Like hatchlings, they are born and raised in the same place, their villages.

But sometimes they venture out for a time, depending on their callings.

North Wind's calling is to become a shaman among the Mandans, much as his own father was. A shaman, I gather, is a person who is somewhat like Melonokus was in the history of Saurius Prime. Melonokus saw things the rest of us did not: other realities, other possibilities for living. Indeed, it was largely thanks to his then-outlawed ideas and visions that our planet's Bloody Tendon Wars drew to a close and an armistice was reached between the carnivores and herbivores.

It was our great King Temm who signed that armistice. He then vanished, with Melonokus, who was never seen again. When Temm reappeared, he had the rules for Cacklaw with him.

Cacklaw is the Saurian game that has replaced war on our planet. I miss it. I haven't top-stomped in a while.

Nika-tc, the lingo-spot whispers, like a second voice.

Yes.

* * *

"Just my luck!" North Wind is yelling. He points to some other mammals now joining the buffalo: horses, who have ridden out from the low rising hills. Riding on these horses are two more mammals — humans, symbiotic with the horses, wrapped in shaggy buffalo skins no longer worn by their original owners.

The humans hold long sticks. They may have seen us. They seem to be riding our way for a visit.

"Run!" North Wind wants me to follow.

"But who are they?"

"The hunters! Crow's Eye!"

"Perhaps, if this Crow's Eye finds me, I could teach him Cacklaw instead. Then he wouldn't try to be a war maker."

"*Warrior.* And it doesn't mean he wants a whole war. Just a small one with you. I told you, he believes it will bring him great honor to find the lizard man that the fur trader Banglees spoke of. But I do not intend to have the vision of my vision quest killed by some swaggering Hidatsa before I am made a shaman!"

The horses are getting closer. I can hear the

yelling of the riders in the distance. One of them aims his long stick in our direction.

"If you expect to be my totem, my power animal, you can't be captured or killed by somebody else. You can't keep letting other people see you. Like that fur trader, Banglees. When he stopped by the lodge fire, all he could talk about was the lizard man who had saved him. If he hadn't been a Frenchman, they might have made *him* shaman."

Just then, a couple of smaller sticks land in the snow near us. Parts of little Earth birds, the feathers, sprout out of one end. Why would you transplant bird feathers to a little jabberstick?

Unless, perhaps, you were trying to insure that the jabberstick had as long a flight as possible?

"Arrows," North Wind says.

The buffalo-covered horse riders are shouting and whooping. One has put his long stick away and grips a kind of stringed instrument, pulling the bow back—to play a note?—with an arrow notched across it. He lets go and the jabberstick comes flying at us. I jump. It barely misses North Wind's head.

Everything was so quiet and peaceful, covered in the snow. I had plenty of time for ice lenses and theorems. How did this suddenly turn into such a sharp, edgy day? But then, mammals are unpredictable.

"Many Lights," North Wind says urgently, "go."

North Wind gave me the name Many Lights because of what he describes as a "vision of color" dancing in the air when I appeared to him. I believe it had more to do with localized temporal displacement, but I like the name. On Saurius Prime, once you leave the nest, you are given your name, and it doesn't change. Agreeing to be known as Many Lights now would be breaking rules from home.

"Many Lights!"

But what could the harm be in having a different name for a while?

Perhaps I really am becoming an outlaw.

More arrows. One hits my tail. My *tail*! That

hurts! I am able to shake it out and pick up North Wind in my arms. It is harder to get a good jump off the soft snow, but the horse-warriors are close and I have to try.

"No! Save yourself, Many Lights—"

North Wind wants me to go. But if I am part of somebody's vision quest, which sounds at least as critical as a school project, I can't just leave him. I gather him up just as the next volley of arrows skim by. I jump, land in the snow, almost drop North Wind, but don't. However, I've jumped toward the crest of the Spirit Mound, right at a patch of freeze-blanket that has been in direct sun all afternoon. It is a little squishy.

Landing, I sink right in to my belly line. Luckily, the horses are having trouble, too. Did those warriors ask the horses if this battle-hunt was all right with them? Do mammals check with other mammals about these things? And does giving North Wind a ride make me a kind of horse?

I struggle out of the squishy snow, preparing to leap over the summit of the Spirit Mound and down the other side, where I calculate that the shadows should make for an icier, firmer surface. I should be able to gain more distance from our pursuers.

"Many Lights—"

I tense and jump, though the softness of the freeze-blanketed surface hampers my liftoff. I manage to get both myself and North Wind to the other side of the mound. We seem to be clear of the horses and the hunters now, or at least we should be. Yet I still hear a horse close by, which seems strange, because they were behind us when—

Oh. I see what North Wind Comes was trying to warn me about. There is another horse. In front of us.

On top, there sits another young man with long black hair like North Wind, but with more colors painted on his face and more feathers in his hair. And not too much buffalo cousin wrapped around his body. He's showing lots of bare mammal skin. As if he enjoys the cold. Or perhaps is challenging it.

We've been driven right to him. Trapped.

Bad Cacklaw move for me.

The ice under my feet continues to crack. Like glass. Like frail lenses.

> *Always riding out*
> *Never coming home*
> *The trail takes me far*
> *Blood and honor*
>   *dancing*

The man on the horse is singing a song as he slowly takes out a bow of his own.

"Crow's Eye," my shaman friend says. "Crow's Eye has found us."

Crow's Eye notches a jabberstick and is about to shoot one now. From this distance, he won't miss.

I am too young for this to happen. Who will there be to report the findings about slow pox and plasmechanics?

Crow's Eye pulls the bow, and the ground below us starts to roar. And opens up.

Chapter Eight

Eli: Journals

June 8: A jentle brease proves a welcome companyun on the second month of our great journey . . .

Error. Suggest: "gentle." Error. Suggest: "grease" or "breeze."

Error. Suggest: "company," "companion," or "comparison." Suggest: Use Language Options menu if attempting to write in a language other than English.

. . . much of which I have undertook in a canoo, these past weeks . . .

Error. Suggest: "can you," "can do," or "cannolli."

It's no use. I may have to write on actual paper. I'm amazed to still have a vidpad at all. It was rolled up and stuffed deep in my pocket and stayed with me all the way from my tumble out of Clyne's ship, through the Fifth Dimension, and back to Earth. It recharges with the sunlight, so I can use it during the day when no one's looking.

But even with power, it doesn't seem to be working right.

<Override spell-check function>

Suggest: Maintain spell-check function.

It's like the vidpad is refusing to do what I ask. It's designed to handle being stuffed in a pocket, but maybe not if that pocket keeps going through different dimensions and times. I mean, now it won't even let me override the spell checker. Which out here will be a real problem.

Everyone is keeping a journal: Clark, Lewis, and a few other men, like Patrick Gass. Gassy has been showing me some of his writing: *We should be respeckted . . .*

Suggest: "respected."

. . . if we return. For we have been both brave & foolish, and will have many tales to tell.

They all want to tell their tales, record their own histories. Who can blame them? With no vidnews, no Comnet, how is anybody else supposed to know what they're doing? Or what they've done, after it's over? How will anyone find out?

Only problem is, none of them can spell really well. I don't know for sure if spelling has been invented yet, but I'm trying to write down some of their versions of words so I can remember them when we return.

If we return. Like Gassy says.

Canoo **[Also suggest: "cannot"]** came from Lewis, and Clark wrote *speshul* **[Suggest: "specious"]** for *special*, and there are tons more like that, including all the versions of words Gassy is coming up with.

If I ever find myself in school again, I'm going to mention these guys whenever a teacher gets upset about how I do on a spelling test.

But school—and everything else I know, even

the Danger Boy stuff—seems a long way off now. I'm not even sure how much time has passed in my world, my real world, my home. I don't know how my father is. Or whether he managed to locate my mom.

Actually, I'm growing less and less sure about which world, which time, really is my own, anyway.

In this world, we've been gone, out in the then-unknown, a couple of weeks. We're into June, and it's summer everywhere out here in the country.

What am I saying? It's *all* "out here in the country." Even what I saw of St. Louis was more like a midsize town at most and not what we think of as a city. The country isn't "out" there. It's everywhere around us. On both sides of the river.

And the river itself.

I go back and forth between riding in the keelboat and riding in the canoe with Gassy or Kentuck. Sometimes, I walk along shore with Lewis and his dog, Seaman. We've seen amazing sights: tall, waving grasses; endless hills; flowers that I don't recognize, sprouting up all over; and a nearly impossible number of animals. It's hard to believe this many animals ever existed outside a zoo. I've seen elk grazing by the shore, fish jumping out of the water, a bobcat mom and her cubs looking for food, deer eating berries and leaves, and even a pair of foxes that stood and looked at us before scooting away.

Like maybe humans weren't something they see every day. Or have to be afraid of yet.

Seaman keeps barking all the time, so maybe we'd see even more animals if he didn't scare them.

The sky is filled with birds. Filled with them. One time, I thought we were having an eclipse. "Pigeons," York told me. "Make good pies, if you catch 'em. And God made so many, people can be eatin' those pies from here to Judgment Day, and the sky is still gonna be full of those birds."

He was talking about passenger pigeons. I know about those. I remember them from when I was in school. They don't exist anymore. That last one died over a hundred years before I was born.

There is so much . . . nature out here, that it feels more like a Comnet game than anything else. It's as fantastic, really, as anything in Barnstormers.

Which is good, because since there is no Comnet, my vidpad is useless for any kind of gaming. But I'm getting ideas for new characters: "The Buffaloner"—half man, half buffalo, all loner. A cleanup hitter who's the last of his kind, drifting from town to town, looking for a team to play with, an outcast even among Barnstormers.

The real buffalo are pretty awesome. Huge, and shaggy, like a force of nature all by themselves. A kinda slow-moving force. We see them more and more often as we head upriver.

Of course, not all of this nature stuff is so great. I've had ticks under my skin, and they only came out when one of the guys burned them with a piece of charcoal from the campfire. And we all have constant—and I mean all the time— mosquito bites.

The bites have made everybody crazy at one time or another. Sometimes we can't sleep, and Seaman's even been driven to howling. The "skeeters," as Kentuck calls 'em, have gotten him all over his nose and ears.

"Hey, young Eli, grab a hold of this — we're gonna push over to shore and get out for a while."

It's York. I'm on the keelboat now, and he wants me to grab one of the long poles that are used for what they like to call steering. Basically, all you do is push against the bottom of the river and send the boat in whatever direction you want to go. The poles are handy when the boat is stuck near a sandbar, but they only work when the water is shallow enough.

I wonder what these guys would think about a digital system that lets you steer by getting signals back from satellites?

"We're gonna look for some game for tonight," York tells me, as I step over with him to the boat's starboard side — that's a sailing word I learned from Clark that means the right side, if you're looking toward the front. And it's the side closest to shore right now.

When York says "game," he's talking about deer or elk or maybe one of those buffalo that we've been spotting.

"Course, you're lookin' like maybe some other things out here consider *you* the game." He's pointing to my arms, which are covered in mosquito bites.

At first, when the ticks and skeeters started to chew me up, I got really scared. What about West Nile virus? Dengue fever? River blindness?

What about slow pox?

But none of the guys had ever heard of those things. Then I remembered that in the days before global warming, diseases all had separate homes—the shifting weather hadn't let them spread all over the place yet, like in 2019.

If anyone here in the Corps of Discovery knew what was coming, would they do anything different to change it? Head it off?

Could they do anything? Can the future really be changed?

Isn't that why the government and Mr. Howe want to turn me into Danger Boy, so that, somehow, the future can be more controllable?

"I like the quiet out here," York says. "I like bein' away from most people. What about you?"

Since there are about seven billion people living on the Earth I come from, I've never seriously considered the question.

In my time, it's hard to get away—from people, or viruses.

"Castor! Castor!"

York and I are pulling the boat to shore, and one of the men who's gone ahead is holding up a dead beaver by its tail, pretty happy about his kill.

"Castor!"

It's Pierre Cruzatte, one of the main boatmen. He's half French and half Indian. Besides hunting and steering boats, he plays his fiddle a lot at night by the campfire. I had never heard of any of the songs he plays. I wonder if he makes them up.

Maybe he'll make one up tonight about dead beavers. *Castor mort.* See, I picked up a few words. Cruzatte likes to talk a lot during the day. He also seems to only see well out of one of his eyes, but he's still able to steer the boats pretty well.

As for *castor mort,* well, there's a lot of *mort* in my time, at least when it comes to animals. There aren't too many beaver or buffalo or bear left out in the once-wild parts. People and bugs have mostly taken over. I never even thought about it much until I wound up here.

The problem with all these animals now, though—like that beaver that's been caught and killed—is that they're going to expect me to eat it later. And when I start to think about it, my stomach starts acting funny.

"Hey, where are you—?"

But I don't have time to answer York's question. As soon as we're close to shore, I jump out and run into the bushes.

Most of what they have to eat here is meat— any kind of meat. They hunt it, skin it, and stew it. Pretty much anything they can get their hands on: deer, birds, snakes, all kinds of fish, gophers (I think), and, lately, more buffalo.

I asked Lewis once if he'd ever heard of people eating veggie dogs.

"Dogs?" Lewis pointed to Seaman. "You wish to eat my dog? He's right there. But we're not that desperate yet, and I'd hate to break a promise to the shaggy fellow."

It seemed like a joke, but you couldn't always tell with Lewis.

Either way, meat wasn't doing to his stomach

what it did to mine. And I don't mean just a bite or two. I mean big heaping piles of cooked meat two or three times a day.

And nobody worried too much about side dishes.

I've been burping a lot on this trip. And worse. Like now.

Once, when my stomach was queasy, Clark tried to give me a shot of whiskey. That only succeeded in burning my throat and almost making me throw up.

At the moment, sitting in the bushes, it's not stuff erupting from my mouth I'm worried about. I try to get comfortable — as comfortable as possible — to take care of my business without getting my butt or legs all scratched or bitten.

There are definitely some places you don't ever want to get bit.

I guess using this vidpad means I'm keeping a kind of journal, too, just like Gassy, Lewis, Clark — like a lot of them. And since a journal is supposed to be a truth-telling place, I need to write about something that happened earlier today. It's connected to the whole food thing.

As I said before, Lewis likes to walk along the shore a lot, sometimes with Seaman alongside since the keelboat and pirogues move so slowly.

Suggest: "peruse."

He can walk along and make notes, sketch birds, take plant samples, and, as he says, "chart longitude and latitude for the maps and settlements to come."

"You already know where the cities will be?" I asked, before realizing the question may have given too much away.

"Cities?" He laughed. "Cities like Philadelphia? Like Richmond, Virginia? Why, even if we survive this expedition, these wild lands won't be settled for hundreds of years. No, young squire, I'm talking about very small outposts, leaving people all the room they'll ever need out here in the Far West."

"Alors!"

Suggest: "aloe" or "allow."

It was Cruzatte again. Usually those shouts

meant that some new animal had been shot. Given he's only got the one good eye, I just hope Cruzatte's aim is careful and he doesn't shoot one of us. I've seen some of his shots ping trees and branches.

"Regardez!"

Suggest: "regalia."

He was asking the rest of us to come take a look at whatever it was.

"Let's go," Lewis said. I hurried along with him, through the cottonwoods and willows (Lewis and some of the others were teaching me how to identify the different kinds of trees), and then we saw it, too: not just the endless stretch of prairie and grassland—all of which would be long gone and turned into suburbs and corn-fields before I was born—but buffalo.

Not a whole herd. Not yet, anyway. But three buffalo standing on the edge of the tall grass, chewing and looking at us.

"We eat good tonight!" Cruzatte said, aiming his gun. They all had these long rifles that you had to stuff full of gunpowder, down into the barrel. And you could only get off one shot at a time.

Lewis had the most advanced gun. He called it an air rifle. It fired like a normal gun, I guess. You could just pull the trigger, as long as there was something in it. You didn't have to stuff the barrel first, anyway.

Cruzatte lifted his rifle and turned to Lewis. "You, monsieur. One shot with the new gun. You take the animal."

Some of the other soldiers from the Corps had come over to us. One of the regular jobs if you weren't on the boat was to hunt along the banks for food.

"Shoot one, sir," one of the soldiers said. "Do the honors. You'll be provisioning us for a week!"

"Indeed."

Of the three buffalo, two were humongous — like the kind you see in zoos. The other one was smaller. It wasn't a baby, but it wasn't as big as the others, either. Maybe a teenager?

Maybe it wasn't much older than me. In buffalo years.

"The lad hasn't had a shot this whole expedition," Lewis said. "Let him." And without even asking, he handed the air gun to me.

It wasn't a toy. It was too heavy.

"Pick one out, Master Sands, and aim straight for the head. For maximum mercy."

Mercy, I thought. "But I don't want to kill them," I said. "They're practically extinct!"

Lewis didn't know what that meant. "I should say they're right here, right now, and we need the meat."

"I don't want to kill them."

"Just one."

"I don't want to cause death." My stomach was feeling funny again.

"Death is always over our shoulder, young Sands, just a half step behind life," Lewis said.

The youngest buffalo, with its thick woolly hide and its big flat wide nostrils and round black eyes, stood staring at me.

"I can't. I won't."

"He is a strange boy, eh?" Cruzatte said. Not very helpfully.

"But in death, the bison will help others live. It's a practically optimistic system, if I do say so myself," Lewis added.

Then he raised my hand. The gun was pointing straight at the teenage buffalo, who chewed and looked at me calmly.

"You will be fine," Cruzatte chimed in. "And we, *c'est bon,* will be full."

"Master Sands."

I wanted to close my eyes.

"Just pull the trigger."

I didn't want to do this.

"We all need to eat. Even you."

I didn't . . .

But the shot came, anyway.

I dropped the gun.

Another shot went off.

The men jumped.

And the young buffalo was down, lying on the grass, his tongue lolling to the side, all the calmness—all the everything—slowly slowly draining from his eyes.

Chapter Nine

Thea: Mulberry Row

Clink-clink-clink.

I follow the hammer sounds down the dirt road outside Jefferson's house. His great home on top of this forested hill: Monticello.

And like all great homes, many people are required to tend to its rhythms and needs, the many wants of the building, and its inhabitants.

Many of those people live right outside the house itself—in a string of small clapboard buildings called Mulberry Row. In Eli's English, they're called shacks—and this is where the slaves live.

Whole families dwell in one or two rooms,

crowded together, laboring, growing Jefferson's crops, making clothes, doing laundry, fabricating construction material so that more of Monticello may be refined and built.

Clink-clink.

I am looking for the one they call a blacksmith.

One who works shaping metals.

A man named Isaac.

Clink.

He fashions building fasteners — nails — out of raw metals. And he makes shoes, too. For horses.

I am here to see one horse in particular.

Clink.

A small boy standing in a doorway waves at me. His mother, who is washing something in a large tub, pulls him back inside. I am considered the "new slave" here. The other slaves don't know if they can trust me yet.

I have learned a few things: I have learned that Jefferson is considered a "good" master, compared to many others, because he doesn't beat his workers or whip them. Still they are not free. Unwhipped or not, they cannot *choose* whether to be here.

Clink!

The boards on these shacks are loose, compared to Jefferson's own grand home. I wonder how cold these people get in winter. Or at night. Fortunately, it's been warm lately.

Or maybe that's just me. The hot flashes, actually, are why I'm on my way to see a horse.

Clink-clink ting!

Sooysaa. Ever since I fell and tangled with him, the wagon-horse has been reported as acting strangely, or "touched," as Sally says.

He's touched, certainly. With a lingo-spot.

I need to see what the effects are.

Clink ting.

Show me . . .

I brush at my ear, like there's a fly buzzing there, but of course there isn't.

The horse grew so unpredictable, they moved him from the main stables out here, behind the blacksmith's on Mulberry Row. Since the animal was potentially dangerous, they decided to let the slaves deal with him.

Did the idea of slaves get invented in the first place when someone realized life had suddenly become too complex, too much for one person, or one family, to handle on their own?

So you force someone else to help handle it for you.

"Can I help you, miss?"

I had followed Sally's instructions. I was at the last building on the row, with the wooden fence behind it.

"I'm looking for Isaac."

"That's me. You have permission to be out here by yourself?"

Sally said Isaac actually grew up with Jefferson. His family was "inherited" by Jefferson President from his own father. In other words, the slaves are treated just like horses.

"I don't want no problem with no runaway on my hands. I don't want no blame for nothin'."

What's he so scared of? I've just come to look at a horse.

"You're that runaway slave girl, right?"

"No. No slave," I tell him, with my newly practiced English.

"What do you mean, 'no slave'?"

I don't try to answer. I see the horse I've come

for. He's tied to a post in the small stable area behind Isaac's workspace. Even in the shadows, I can see the animal is still scared, pulling against the bridle ropes that keep it tied to the fence.

Poor thing. If the lingo-spot is working, it's probably overwhelmed with information.

"No slave." I repeat absently, making my way toward the horse.

"Really, you shouldn't—" He's almost pleading with me, but I don't listen.

Then another voice starts up. Someone ahead of me. In the shadows.

"No slave but Brassy."

I recognize the speaker.

It's Mr. Howard. He's waiting for me by the horse.

No wonder Isaac seemed so nervous.

Howard probably told him I wanted the horse because I was trying to escape.

I probably should tell him I *am* escaping, though I'm not. It would make more sense than the truth. But why talk at all? He'll grab me at any moment, so I have to focus on the horse.

"Sooysaa . . ."

The animal flicks its head in my direction, eyes widening.

Show me . . .

Show me what?

Howard is advancing toward me, the same wild look on his face that he's had ever since trying on Eli's cap. He takes a whip off a nearby post.

Horses are whipped to control their behavior. And so are slaves who are caught trying to escape. That's what I was told, though it hasn't happened to me, so far.

I've had a couple of days of rest and recovery here, at Jefferson President's estate. After my fall from the horse, they wanted to make sure none of my bones were broken. I suppose there was some genuine concern there. "But they also have to return you to Louisiana's governor in one piece," Sally told me. "They want the merchandise to be in good condition."

Unless I can find a way to leave this place, I am apparently to be sent to this territorial governor within the week. No wonder Mr. Howard thinks I'm trying to escape. He's been telling Jefferson to have me watched more closely and to stop leaving me alone with Sally.

"All of America appears gripped by fevers and fugue states," Jefferson said in response to one of Howard's warnings. "At least, all of Monticello does. It would behoove you to be sure of your facts."

He often said such things in Latin, for my benefit. He imagines I understand him and is intrigued by that. Or amused.

"She will be wasted on that governor," he said.

Apparently, if one is a slave, one is better off amusing the master than angering him, and better off still being thought of as particularly useful. None of it flatters me.

Jefferson's use of the Roman tongue does allow me to listen more intently with my actual ears, while trying to tune out the lingo-spot. More and more, the Saurian translation device seems to be creating a type of noise that can become quite disturbing. Like an unbidden thought that startles you.

As it did during my carriage ride with Sally. It's as if the spot were becoming an extra mind to direct my own. I have tried to remove it, putting the residue in a small crystal jar I retrieved from the cooking quarters. Honoré, Jefferson's chef, was there, standing by the long wooden tables and knocking carved spoons over large iron pots.

"Get out! I am busy! Can you not see?"

"I need—"

"I have been ordered to sabotage perfectly good *fromage* on another of Monsieur Jefferson's experiments, and if he has sent you here to tell me about another *idée* he has for an *entrée*, well, *mon Dieu!* It will have to—"

"I just need a jar," I said. In Latin. He didn't understand.

"Can you not speak *français?*" he asked, but after I gestured with hand signals, he let me take what I wanted.

I want to preserve the lingo-spot in order to examine it later, when I get back. But back to where? Eli's home? K'lion's? Certainly not mine.

Mine's been burned.

The most startling effect of the lingo-spot

happened shortly after I was brought here and put to bed to recover from my bruises suffered in the fall. Evidently I not only slept deeply but also experienced a kind of "waking trance," according to what Jefferson President and Sally told me later.

This was one of the "fugue states" Jefferson made reference to. While in it, he said, I "talked so vividly, it was as if you'd actually lived in ancient Egypt." I resisted the urge to tell him, "I did."

But what did he mean by "ancient"?

In the lingo-spot vision, I had been with my mother, Hypatia. I was lying on a marble bench, covered in a light cotton cloth, shivering with fever. "Mermaid," she said to me softly, using her favorite nickname for me. "Mermaid. You are not yourself." She smiled. She took a pitcher of lemon juice, honey, and water, and she dribbled a little on my lips.

"Come back, Mermaid."

"Where—where have I been?" I managed to ask her. "And . . . what am I becoming?"

She looked at me and just kept smiling. I wanted to kiss her, to thank her for a lifetime of touching, of whispered love. For warm food and lazy naps and needed healing. For letting me see her in her sadnesses and rages, and letting me know she still loved me then, too.

I wanted to do all that, and it felt—in that vision—like that balmy afternoon stretched infinitely in front of me, giving me all the time I'd ever need.

You always think you'll have all the time you'll ever need.

Show me . . .

But you don't.

Show me . . .

And yet it was so vivid to me, it was as if the lingo-spot were trying to show me . . . the things I really meant to say, if I only had a chance. . . .

As if its task had now become a different kind of translation, that of making a deeper self known, intelligible, to me.

But when I woke, I was in Jefferson President's house, still a slave named Brassy who was supposed to be returned to the one who "owns" her.

"Show me . . ." I whisper to the horse as I draw close.

The animal is frightened. According to the

rumors I kept hearing in the house, the one I call Sooysaa has been fearful ever since the accident. In Alexandria, people often regarded sudden skittish behavior in their animals as an augury of some human disaster.

Sooysaa was acting spooked, haunted. Jefferson even mentioned having the animal destroyed.

I had to find out if I could help it. If I talked to it, calmed it, then maybe it wouldn't have to be killed. There's been too much death around me lately.

But, of course, I couldn't tell anyone any of this. Especially not if they're all insisting I'm really this —

"Brassy!"

I won't answer to the slave name. I step toward the horse, but out of the corner of my eye, I see Howard stepping over the stacks of hay, holding the whip, and it's hard not to flinch.

"Here, Sooysaa." I'm trying to keep the horse calm. "Don't be scared." I just want to get close enough to whisper a single question to it before I'm hauled away.

I see now that the horse is also restrained by chains around two of its ankles. Otherwise, it would bolt.

"Easy, Sooysaa."

Mr. Howard's right behind me.

"I'm not trying to run away," I tell him, without turning around.

I don't say it in English, so he doesn't understand. In fact, my speaking at all—in a foreign tongue, no less—seems to make him even angrier.

Then the whip *cracks.*

And lands on the horse.

"Obey!" Howard hisses.

And again on the animal.

Sooysaa is screaming, kicking against his stall with his free legs.

Crack!

This time the whip lands on me.

The pain is stunning: the leather coil has sheered off some of my skin above the shoulder.

Howard is getting ready to land another blow.

"Mr. Howard. Stand down."

It's Jefferson. He stands in the rear with Sally and Isaac.

"No more hurt. No more hurt."

Another voice. Near me. But I feel it, more than hear it.

Show me . . .

Sooysaa. Yes. A lingo-spot that can translate . . . emotion . . . wouldn't require a specific language to work. On animals. Or anyone else.

"No more hurt."

It's the horse.

"No more."

I can feel blood start to run down my arm.

The horse and I are talking. Both thinking we're about to explode, or go under, from the feelings inside.

Mr. Howard stands nearby, the whip raised, uncertain whether to strike or not.

"You will not hurt the girl, Mr. Howard. She is the new governor's property, after all, and she's in our care now."

I'm nobody's property. But if it keeps another blow from landing, I'll let the comment pass. For now.

Sally walks over to me. She has a rag, which she touches gently against my shoulder.

"Horse," I tell her. In English. "Horse. Much scared."

"Who can blame it, child?" Sally says. "It's a frightening world for a horse." She looks at Jefferson. "We need to get this one back inside."

She means me, since the horse isn't going anywhere.

"She was trying to escape. Sir," Howard says, in an attempt to explain his actions, "it would hardly do to allow the governor's property to disappear."

"When I need your counsel on slave matters, Mr. Howard, I shall ask it. Please prepare my carriages. I can no longer put off my return to Washington, and I fear we must return there in the morning." Then he turns to Isaac. "I am sorry for this interruption in your commendable duties, Isaac."

Isaac nods but doesn't say anything.

Howard quickly fills the silence. "She's a danger, sir. I can feel it."

"Your feelings are duly noted, Mr. Howard. But I have use of her now, in my study. I find she may help in solving a scientific anomaly I have come across in my research."

"It would give the other slaves bad ideas, sir, if they see her doing that. Especially when they know she deserves to be punished. What would the governor say if you allow her such privilege?"

"The governor, I am sure, will want his runaway well-mended when we hand her over. Even if she is high-spirited. And frankly, Mr. Howard, as long as she can answer a couple of questions about the mathematician Hypatia and the library at Alexandria, I am willing to risk whatever the governor might say."

Hypatia!

Mother.

Then maybe Jefferson President knows who I really am after all.

And where I really belong.

Chapter Ten

Clyne: Spirit Mound

"We have to get you out of here, before the little people get us." It's North Wind Comes.

We are someplace dark. I can hear but can't see well. And my leg hurts. I'm not sure why. If I ever get back to Saurius Prime, I'm seeing the student nurse before I deliver any findings.

"Is it awake now?"

That's *not* North Wind Comes.

"He's not an *it*. He's a good spirit. A helpful vision."

Click. A new sound.

"Well, there's little honor in killing him like this, in the dark, when he can't even see me. Can you heal him? Get him moving again. Then, at least, it would be a hunt."

Click. Click.

Who's speaking? Why does my leg hurt so much? I reach out . . . there's blood on my leg limb. My blood.

This perhaps can't wait for school nurses.

This perhaps reminds me, I may never get home at all.

Still feeling my *gra-baaked* limb, I notice a *perpendicular part* of that lower leg that was never there before. Sticking out. Like a bone.

"Ow! Ow! Ow!"

"Be careful, Many Lights."

"You've given him a name? A demon? A *name*?"

North Wind Comes doesn't respond to the other human mammal. "You are hurt, Many Lights. Crow's Eye hit you."

A jabberstick! That's a jabberstick in my leg!

It's not a bone. I wonder if that qualifies as "good news"?

"And I did a fairly dishonorable job of it. Wounding, not killing." *Click snkkk.*

So that's Crow's Eye in the darkness, next to us.

"Personally, although I am literally at pains to say it, I prefer a mere wound to the alternative."

The clicking stops. "He speaks. You didn't tell me he speaks."

"You didn't ask."

Click. Now a spark follows the noise. *Click.* Another. *Click-click.* And another. Crow's Eye has been striking two rocks together. I can see that now, because one of the sparks has caught in some straw and started a small fire. He blows on it. The fire grows.

"I think we will have heat now." As the fire grows orange — citrus-colored and warm, though there's little sweet about any of this — I get a closer look at Crow's Eye's face. It is brown-red like North Wind's, somewhat like Thea's, with very black eyes, and a kind of scowl. But it's still a young face, and the attempt to hold on to that fierce look, regardless of what he may be heart-experiencing underneath, makes him look like a youthful Cacklaw rear guard trying a head fake on new opposition.

Thanks to the light from his fire, however, I can now not merely feel, but *see* the jabberstick in my leg.

North Wind points to it. "Your arrow, Crow's Eye."

"Yes, North Wind, that is my arrow, sticking out of your demon friend. I suppose, since we are trapped here, I should just wait for him to die from blood loss and then drag him to the village, like an old woman who has found a beached trout and brings it back as if she's a great hunter. Then again, we will be lucky if an old woman finds us here at all and fetches help. My life as a warrior is over before it has begun. Instead, I will be like Coyote, chasing my own tail, acting like a fool."

"I always thought Coyote offered much wisdom," North Wind says. "In his own crazy way."

"Then perhaps I should offer myself as an assistant to a Mandan shaman-in-training, cheering up his patients before he works his wonders."

Crow's Eye isn't happy at all. You don't even need to hear his words. With just the small light we have, you can see it in the way shadows move across his face.

"Crow's Eye. Look around," North Wind says. He's not happy, either. "We can't wait for old women, or young girls, or the rest of your raiding party, or anybody else. We have to get out of here now."

Yes, we do. Because I have brought some plasmechanical material to this world that has become infected, and if left untended, it could make life even more unpredictable for these mammals than they make it themselves.

I also have to find time, away from Crow's Eye, to warn my friend that the gift I thought I was giving him—the gift of understanding, from the lingo-spot—may be doing things to his body.

Or his mind.

But first there is the problem of the jabberstick jutting out of my leg. And how we all got in here in the first place.

"Thank you, yes," I say, trying to mimic at least a faint cheerfulness. "My jumping limb is aching fiercely, I have lost more blood than I am comfortable with sparing, and if you could keep me awake, I'm sure I can guide one of your medical practitioners through the proper care and suturing of Saurian wounds."

As the Saurian elders are fond of saying, *You must count to one before you reach two.* No need to wait for a far-off school nurse or even the lucky old woman that Crow's Eye mentioned, who might be looking for us. I will simply use the first-aid training I learned as a vacation-time assistant in the play area for nestlings, back on Saurius Prime, and guide one of these mammals in the true healing arts.

That is, I would if either of them were paying attention to me.

In the dim light, Crow's Eye finds something scattered on the ground that intrigues him, and he begins grabbing it up by handfuls.

"Now do you believe me, North Wind? The devils that live here are not as harmless as you would wish." Crow's Eye clutches a fistful of raw bones. Some are bleached with age. Others have been more recently gnawed.

The bones are everywhere. Bones and skulls and dried bits of skin and fur. You'd think the Bloody Tendon Wars had just been fought here. Except, most of these remains are mammal.

I am the only injured Saurian.

"Perhaps, North Wind Comes, you should use your shaman magic to get us out of here."

North Wind doesn't answer right away, so I take the opportunity to ask what I think is a sensible question under the circumstances:

"Mammal men, how did we get inside the Spirit Mound?"

I'm feeling a bit strange, lightheaded.

Arrak-du.

Lost lands up ahead.

"It happened, Many Lights, right after we ran into Crow's Eye's trap. The ice, the snow, had frozen over an opening. Your jumping, and the horse's stomping, caused great cracks to appear. We might have escaped the cave-in had not Crow's Eye's arrow hit you just before the collapse."

"I had dismounted and was going to finish you off myself," Crow's Eye adds. "Perhaps it's still not such a bad idea. I will find my way out of here and take this demon's body back to the Mandans, to let them see where their shamans draw their power."

"You misconstrue, war mammal," I say, attempting to gently correct him. "Any power North Wind has is his own. Do you think you could cut this jabberstick out of my limb now?"

In the firelight, I could see Crow's Eye staring at me in amazement. I had switched from speaking Mandan to the particulars of the Hidatsa tongue. I don't know if that was the reason he was starting to look even more upset. Or perhaps it was because I was asking him to undo his handiwork with the jabberstick.

"I trust I must have blacked out during the fall," I say.

"Only briefly." North Wind is working his way over to me, now that he can see me. Perhaps as a means of keeping Crow's Eye at bay.

"Crow's Eye, if we are in a trap set by devils, then the dishonor of being caught so easily would scarcely be offset by killing the lizard man."

Crow's Eye considers this observation, then says, "Is that the only mind-trick you have, shaman-to-be? Trying to use words to change my purpose?"

"His blood," North Wind adds, "will only draw the devils to us."

"But there are no devils. That's just a story for children and shamans. A warrior wouldn't really believe such things."

"You just spoke of them," North Wind says.

North Wind and Crow's Eye continue their debate. No one is paying much attention to my steady blood loss, or worrying about the eventual effects of necrosis on my wounded extremity.

Nor are they worried at all, as am I, that a technology from another planet has been infected with a disease from another era, which may affect their world far more than small devils, diminutive spirit beings, or tribal rivalries between jittery mammals.

I look around in the expanding firelight and see better the remains around us. I can also see that while neither of my two companions has to contend with protruding jabbersticks, the fall into the void has been hard on their bodies as well.

"We need to leave this place," North Wind

says, deciding that will end his half of the devil argument.

"Yes. Well, my horse is still up there, in the world," Crow's Eye replies, pointing. "Outsmarting all of us by avoiding this fall. Perhaps you could call him and he'll fly down to us."

North Wind doesn't answer him. There's no horse and no flying, but all of a sudden there's considerable movement, the flickers of many shadows, and breathing.

A lot of breathing.

Glinting just out of range of the firelight, there are many pairs of eyes staring at us from the darkness beyond. I don't know if these are the devils that North Wind and Crow's Eye were arguing about.

But now we have company.

Chapter Eleven

Eli: Good Humor Island

The last time I had a gun in my hand felt like a lifetime ago. Or at least a couple of months. It was Clark's rifle, and he wanted me to shoot a buffalo.

The buffalo was shot, all right.

It turned out Floyd—Kentuck—was coming up behind us, and he was firing, practically right over my shoulder. It was a dangerous thing to do, but he was a good aim.

Floyd's dead now. Just like the buffalo. But with Kentuck, it wasn't a gun. He fell sick and died in August.

We'd been going upriver, sketching the animals, counting the fish, pulling the boats, swatting the mosquitoes. It took so long to get anywhere. How did people do anything except stay home?

Were Thea and Clyne on journeys like this, too?

"My stomach ain't right," Kentuck said to me one afternoon.

"I think it's all this meat," I told him. "It's like being stuck on some crazy grownup fad diet."

But it never got righter. He couldn't keep any food down and he kept shaking from a fever. This went on for a couple weeks or so.

The last couple days, we'd stopped completely to let him rest. And he just died . . . in the middle of the night.

Me, Clark, and a few of the others were sitting up with him when it happened. "Here," Kentuck said. He took something from under his heavy shirt and tried to press it into my hands. He didn't have much strength. "For good luck."

It looked like a really old, really falling apart, softball of some kind. A leather softball. "What . . . ?"

"Shhh," Clark said. "Looks like he was saving his old Fives ball."

"'Fives'? What is . . . ?"

But Clark held his finger to his lips again. He didn't want to use up the last of Kentuck's strength telling me about some old softball.

It was hard to think of Kentuck with no strength. The same guy who always made jokes with me in the keelboat, or showed me how to cut and skin an animal that's been shot.

That's what we did with the buffalo he killed. Since I was already eating buffalo meat (I still am—it's the main part of our diet now, and it still makes me run off to the bushes sometimes), I decided that maybe I had to take some responsibility . . . for my food. It didn't come in some tidy package from a store, so I couldn't pretend that the "food" had once been anything else but a living, breathing creature.

So when Kentuck had his big knife out that day and asked if I wanted to help, I said yes. He was covered in blood up to his elbow as he cut through the stringy white and pink tendons that kept the "meat"—the young bison's fat and tissue and muscle—connected to its skin and fur.

"You can live all winter sometimes off'n one well-dressed animal, if it's big enough."

"Dressed? I thought we were cutting it up."

Kentuck laughed. I'm not sure if he thought I was making a joke, or if he understood I really didn't know what he meant. It turns out that dressing an animal *is* how you cut up the meat, and how you save the really big pieces—whether you smoke them or cover them in salt—for eating later. Sometimes a lot later.

"Whatever state you said you were from, must be a lot of funny people there." Kentuck smiled. Did I tell him I lived in California? "Here."

He handed me two big handfuls of . . . guts. Guts, stomach, intestines, I'm not sure which. I almost passed out right there, thinking we were going to eat all that. Then I remembered that these were the parts the men usually threw into the river.

"*Très bon pour les poissons!*" Cruzatte said.

Good for the fish. Apparently these guys believed there were a lot of piranhas in the water or something.

But they kept the livers. The men liked cooking up the livers.

Soon I was covered in blood myself. I wasn't happy about it, but if you're going to eat food that used to walk around, you can't keep fooling yourself, either. But I still told the Corps I didn't want to hunt.

Right now, though, there's a gun in my hand, and members of the Corps are telling me to get ready to fire my first shot.

What's even worse is that this isn't a hunt and they don't mean to shoot a buffalo.

They mean, "Fire at a human being when you hear the order."

Basically, I'm expected to murder someone, because we're on the verge of maybe getting murdered ourselves.

We're on a sandbar, in the middle of the Missouri River. Clark has named this little patch Good Humor Island. Across from us is a tribe of Lakota

Indians lined up onshore, with their arrows pointed at us.

Clark is in front of us, with a drawn sword, looking real expedition-leader-like, yelling across the water at a Lakota chief whose name, of all things, is the Partisan.

It's a name for someone who takes a side in a debate, or an argument, or a war. Lewis told me that. It's a funny kind of name and, right now, about the only funny thing at all on Good Humor Island.

In fact, as I stand here holding a rifle that I really have no intention of using, the thought strikes me that the Partisan could be a kind of Barnstormer character—a ghost Indian, haunting people who took his land.

Buffaloner, meet the Partisan.

At the thought of it, I giggle. Everyone— Indian, American, French—stares at me. Right. No laughing on Good Humor Island.

Except maybe for one other rule-breaker: He's a Lakota boy, about my age, holding a bow and arrow, pointed pretty much right at me. I think he's the son of Black Buffalo, one of the other chiefs. He's been watching me the whole time we've been here. Now, I guess, I'm his number-one target in case a war breaks out.

Except that my giggle almost made him laugh, too.

The Lakota, I learned, is a tribe that lives by the river and demands a kind of toll from anyone who passes by. A shipping tax. Even if what's being "shipped" is you.

We just want to get upriver to a place called Mandan Village. It's where we're supposed to be spending the whole winter. We need to be there in a few weeks.

But we're not spending the winter anywhere unless we get off this sandbar. The Corps tried to pay the tax with some knives, an American flag, an old but usable coat, some buffalo meat, and some medals.

Those were the "Great Father Jefferson" medals Lewis and Clark had with them to introduce all the tribes they were meeting to the president, since the idea was that the land now belonged to

America, and the president was going to be the main chief now.

You can imagine how that idea didn't really sit well with anyone who was already living here, with chiefs of their own already picked out.

Plus, the Lakota are smart enough to know that when the American "Great Father" takes over, they'll be out of the shipping-tax business, and they don't want to see a good thing go.

Well, not such a good thing for us in the Corps.

Everyone was edgy and nervous. Maybe the Indians could sense that no matter what they did to us — fired their arrows, or let us pass — it might not really matter. Big journeys change things. Lewis and Clark's journey would change things forever. Eventually tons of people would be pouring into the West, once they knew what was out there. For the Indians, that would be another kind of death.

Maybe the Lakota thought that by killing us, they could just put that particular death off a little while longer.

"I am going away," Floyd had told me, right before he died. "I want you to write me a letter."

I was sitting there, silently, just like Clark wanted me to. Not asking about "Fives" or anything else. I thought Clark wouldn't mind if I asked who Floyd wanted the letter sent to, though.

But Kentuck never got to tell me. I went to find some sheets of paper and one of those feather-quill pens everybody uses. I couldn't use my vid-pad in front of him. Though maybe, if he was dying, why not? It wouldn't mess up history too much for him to have seen it, would it?

Anyway, when I got back to where Floyd was laying, he was gone. Just like that. From nothing more than what seemed like a real bad flu. Lewis called it something else—like that thing babies get—cholera? No—colicky, that's it. *Cholic.*

I didn't know that could kill you.

"We name this river Floyd's River," Clark said at the funeral. We buried him on a hill in a really pretty spot, and the men in the Corps fired off their guns. Cruzatte played a sad fiddle tune, and Seaman howled, so it was an official military event. I'd never been to anyone's funeral before.

"We name this hill Floyd's Bluff. Both will bear his name for ages afterward, and those names will tell of his great deeds. He was a brave and worthy man. And now he's gone."

Clark wasn't a preacher and there didn't seem to be much more to say. He turned to the other captain. "Meriwether?"

Meriwether shook his head. "Kentuck was among the most cheerful of us," he added. "The universe doesn't always reward cheerfulness. Perhaps, in honor of our friend, we should all remain cheerful, out of spite. May God take his soul."

No one said anything else, but really, how could they? They were all trying to figure out what Lewis meant.

Everybody took a turn putting a shovelful of dirt on Kentuck's body. It was wrapped in an American flag, and I could actually see his feet sticking out from it, down in the hole. I put some dirt on him, too.

That must be why there always seems to be a tiny part inside grownups that seems a little sad, because if you live long enough, you see it. You *know.*

People go. Places, things.

You love them, and they still go. Thea knows that now. Look what happened to her mom.

Even being unstuck in time, like I am, you don't get "do overs." Not really. You can't hold on to everything.

Or anything. Sometimes.

Standing on Floyd's Bluff, I couldn't remember from school if anyone on the Lewis and Clark expedition actually died. What if they hadn't, originally? What if I caused that by being here, by changing history?

That's what's going through my head now, here on Good Humor Island, with this big museum gun in my hand, pointed at people I hardly even know. I'm pretty sure Lewis and Clark survived, but what if my changing things means, this time, they don't?

What if things go really wrong in the next few minutes, and a lot of us don't even make it out of here?

"Eli?"

It's York. The Indians seem fascinated by him. They were touching his skin before. They've seen

French fur traders coming down the river, but they've never seen a black man. It's hard to imagine a time in America when having different skin color was unusual.

"What is it, Mr. York?"

"You ready to fire that thing, if you have to?"

"I've never fired a gun before. I've never killed a person."

"Well, me neither."

"And I'm not going to start now! This isn't some Comnet game!"

"Some what?"

On the shore, the Indian boy, with his bow and arrow, is watching me talk to York. You can see his eyes follow us every time we shift positions.

I'd like to throw my gun down, to show how ridiculous I think this all is, but any sudden move like that would get everyone scared, and all those bullets and arrows would go flying. But I wonder, if there was some way to signal a truce to that Lakota kid, would he go along?

I'm not sure how it all went so wrong, anyway. Clark had been going back and forth from our island, giving gifts to the tribe for the last day or two. Maybe it was the "Great White Father" medal that finally rubbed them the wrong way. Or maybe it was when they tasted Lewis's "portable soup." That was probably a mistake, as gifts go.

Clark had ordered us to set off from Good Humor Island, but when we were getting the pirogues ready, the Partisan grabbed the ropes to keep us from leaving.

That's when we noticed all the arrows pointed at us.

Lewis, for his part, calmly got out his air rifle. He explained what it was, the translator told the chiefs, and nobody moved an inch after that. Nobody gave in.

This silence is dangerous. Unless somebody says something soon, shots will go off just from the tension.

Clark must be thinking the same thing. "We are not squaws, but warriors," he says suddenly, out loud.

I'm not sure that's the kind of silence-breaking

that helps. I guess Clark is getting pretty frustrated, too.

Why does he make fun of girls, anyway? Like all girls are scaredy-cats and all boys aren't. That's not true. If they met Thea or her mom, they wouldn't say stuff like that. Or if they met my mom.

Though it doesn't exactly help to think about her right now.

The Lakota translator is telling the Partisan, Black Buffalo, and the others what Clark said. He gets a reply.

"We are not squaws, either."

I get it with my lingo-spot, before our translator — Cruzatte — tells Clark.

Share . . .

What? Share what? Was that me thinking that?

Somebody has to think of *something*, though. These grownups will get us all killed.

What would Kentuck be doing if he were here? Would it have changed our luck if he was still alive?

Kentuck . . .

With my non-rifle hand, I slowly reach into my

pants pocket and pull out the scraggly, leathery Fives ball he'd given me. It feels like every eye in the world is watching me.

I slowly hold up the ball. And then I start to bend over and — slowly, slowly — lay down the rifle on the sand.

Clark and the others are casting glances at me, too, while trying to keep an eye on the Lakota. "Eli? What in thunder are you doing?"

"Trust me, sir."

Showing the Lakota I only have the ball in my hand, I point across the river to the boy. He's confused and looks over to his chiefs for advice. The Partisan just shakes his head no, without knowing what I'm going to do. Black Buffalo, though, holds up his hand in more of a let's-wait-and-see gesture.

I make a sweeping arc with my hand, for practice, without releasing the ball.

I found out at Floyd's funeral that Fives is some kind of handball game. Nothing to do with bats. But Floyd wanted me to have it, anyway. For me, it's become a kind of softball.

Cocking my arm back, I swing forward and

throw it—a nice, easy, underhand pitch—across the water.

It lands at the Lakota kid's feet on the far riverbank. He doesn't know what to do. Black Buffalo looks at the ball, back at me, and then at his son. This time, he nods. The Partisan turns away in a huff.

The kid sets down his bow and arrow and picks up Floyd's ball like I hoped he would. He looks at me, and I mime the throwing gesture. He gets it, and without even practicing, throws the ball over the river, back to me.

We do that one more time. Though after I throw the ball to the Lakota side, I make another deliberate show of picking up a damp piece of willow tree driftwood and holding it aloft.

The Lakota kid is puzzled, but he throws the ball back again.

And now, as the ball comes flying toward me, I swing, make contact, and hit the ball toward the boy and the Lakotas. It falls a little short, landing with a plop in the water near their feet.

Some of them scatter. An arrow whizzes by

overhead. One of the Corps is about to shoot back, and I think, how ridiculous, I've ruined everything by taking an at-bat. Clark is screaming, "No!" and so is Black Buffalo — you can tell, without a translator — but no one else fires, and the kid runs over to where the ball rolls by the river-bank. He picks it up again and turns to look at me . . .

. . . and seems to be smiling.

"What game is that?" Black Buffalo asks.

I'm so excited, I don't wait for the translator and answer, "Baseball!"

Clark and Lewis both give quizzical looks at my evident understanding of Lakota.

"And if this is September," I tell Black Buffalo, "it's just about time for the playoffs."

The Lakota translator is giving me a quizzical look, too. He's never heard anything like that from any of the fur traders.

I see that the Lakota kid is picking up a stick, too. He stands, holding it the way I held mine, but not before tossing the ball back over the water to me.

I guess he's ready for an at-bat.

Men on both sides are lowering their weapons.

It looks like the Corps of Discovery will make it through the day and off of Good Humor Island.

And if that means I've messed with history a little, it feels all right.

Chapter Twelve

Thea: Monticello

We follow Jefferson outside, going back up Mulberry Row.

Sadness . . .

Eyes watch us. There are a few nods, but fewer smiles.

Jefferson occasionally nods back at a slave or two but doesn't stop to make conversation.

. . . sore . . . tired . . .

I don't know who's talking. . . .

No, I do know. No one is talking. The lingo-spot is not only translating words now, but feelings. But which feelings? Maybe . . . the strongest ones?

If this ability should grow, I may well go mad.

And as Mother might have observed, going mad will not help me think clearly about my situation.

The slave cabins are opposite the extensive, and apparently experimental, gardens that Jefferson keeps. Orange light from a setting sun plays over the flowers, trees, and vines there. Looking at them, smelling them, I could almost imagine myself back in the gardens in Alexandria.

Almost.

We're back at the front entrance to the house quickly enough. "Come with me, girl," Sally says, and takes me upstairs.

I noticed she didn't look too closely at the slaves on Mulberry Row, either. She doesn't quite belong there, but she doesn't quite belong here, in Jefferson's house, as a full family member.

Like me, she is caught between worlds.

Two of Jefferson's granddaughters run by, giggling as they see me. Jefferson's grown daughter, Patsy, is here with her family — I don't think I've counted all the young ones yet. There are around six or so. I don't know how they can move so fast in such garments, though, with all the bows and sashes around their waists.

Even the men, those who aren't slaves, seem to wear numerous layers of clothing.

But to be a child is to move fast, no matter what your clothing, so off the children go, perhaps to look at some of the antlers on the wall. This is a busy house, which also reminds me of Alexandria and the library. Something was always happening there. Guests were forever arriving. Back when *I* was a child.

And if I'm not quite a child now, but not yet grown into the sort of woman Mother was . . . then what am I? Who am I?

Honoré stomps by on his way to the kitchen, holding a basket full of peas he's brought in from outside. "And I still have to make ice cream for *tous les petits* Jeffersons!" he yells to no one in particular.

"We'll go up here and wait in the cabinet room."

I follow Sally up the stairs, into what must be Jefferson's study.

Like Mother's, it is strewn with papers and scientific implements of every sort. There is a kind of paddle hanging on the wall. There is a plate of oranges on his desk. The scented fruit reminds me of home. I wonder if he has any lemons.

There's an apparatus on his desk that seems designed for making scrolls. There are sheets of parchment in it, but I'm not sure how it works. Most peculiar of all, though, are several large bones set out on tables, trails of dirt and debris around them.

I believe these may be some of the bones Jefferson brought back from the trip where we found Eli.

Where I found him, only to lose—

Miss.

—him again.

Who said *miss*?

"Jefferson has an active mind," Sally tells me.

I realize I have been staring at the large animal bones. "Mostly that's a good thing. It keeps him busy, keeps all that sadness of his at bay." She shakes her head. "But sometimes it keeps him from paying attention to the things that are right in front of him. To the life he's leading right now."

"Sally, you say the worst things about me. It's scarcely fair."

"Yes, Jefferson, it's scarcely fair."

Jefferson had entered through a side door. He holds a large, musty volume in his hands, a "book" as scrolls are now called.

Even in this quick exchange, I can tell there's a bond between these two, but I can't make sense of it.

"If I believed in Providence, I would say that my continued delay in getting back to Washington is a penalty for having indulged secret travels in the first place. Except that I don't mind the delay at all. However, I expect my political enemies in the Whig Party will not let it be forgotten."

I nod toward Jefferson, just to be agreeable.

"Do you speak much English?" he asks me.

"Some bit," I tell him. I'm surprised to hear myself say it.

"You appeared to understand it in the stables. You've taxed all the Greek and Latin out of me, though I enjoy the practice. It may save time if I can proceed in the common tongue. Is that all right?"

I nod again. I can't tell him about the lingo-spot.

And then it occurs to me that by using English, he's including Sally in the conversation, too.

He's trusting her.

"I am always trying to save time. There never seems to be enough." He pauses at the parchment machine. "For instance, this polygraph I invented. It allows a duplicate to be made of every letter I write. It works by putting a pen in a brace that copies every stroke I make with my own hand."

The scribes in Alexandria could have used that. We would have had extra copies of all our scrolls and perhaps wouldn't have lost them all in the fire.

"These bones," Jefferson says, coming up to the table. "They save no time whatsoever, but I am fascinated by them. I cannot help but wonder what sorts of mighty creatures lived here in America before us. I believe there may have been giants."

He looks at me . . .

Tell me.

. . . to see what I know. He suspects something. "These bones, for example, come from a creature I've been calling the *incognitum* because I have yet to ascertain what species it is. Though, lately, I wonder if it might not be some kind of elephant. I recalled reading that Alexander the Great used elephants for military purposes, then went to find a volume about him that I had procured in Europe. It was richly illustrated, and I hoped the engravings might give me a basis to make a few renderings of our own prehistoric elephants.

"Alexander, of course, founded the great city of Alexandria. The original one, in Egypt. Our smaller, humbler settlement of the same name, here in Virginia, hopes to draw inspiration from its source and someday serve as a seat of learning."

He is still looking at me.

Tell me.

"Jefferson, for this poor girl's sake, come to your point."

"Here is the section of the book on Alexandria." He lets the volume fall open. I see a series of accurate engravings of the great legends of my city: Alexander's arrival, its transformation to a great shipping port, the building of the library, the museum, and Pharos—the great lighthouse. That was the last place I saw my mother alive.

They're all there in Jefferson's book.

"And then there is this brief section about the great fire in Alexandria, and the destruction of its golden age."

He flips the large, moldering pages.

In the engravings, I see the fire taking the library. I see the animals fleeing the zoo on the palace grounds, just as I remember them. I see K'lion.

"I noticed this lizard man in the illustration," Jefferson says, tapping his finger on the pages. "And I do not recall ever seeing him there before. But there was an even bigger surprise waiting for me on the next page."

He takes the bound parchment to reveal another engraving on that page.

> *The mathematician and scholar Hypatia stood accused of consorting with demons and demigods, and this may have led to her downfall.*

The caption is the Gaul language, French, and Jefferson reads it in the original.

"Do you need me to—"

"No," I tell him. I don't need him to translate.

He just shakes his head.

The picture is of Mother. Mother talking to K'lion.

It never happened, but somehow the author of this book thinks it did. Somehow, a version of our story has made its way down through the ages.

"You mentioned Hypatia's name during your restless sleep. You called her 'Mother.'"

"Jefferson, this child's clearly upset. She's still weak. What are you—"

"I am beginning to wonder, Sally, if I've made a serious mistake letting that boy join the Corps of Discovery to capture the lizard man. I am beginning to wonder if the West may hold such mysteries that the entire country may come undone. And I certainly wonder how a bound and printed book is able to alter its very illustrations."

Sally is getting upset.

"You need to leave this girl be, Tom!"

Jefferson's eyes widen.

"Not everything that passes in front of your eyes is something to be used in an experiment or examined like some bug!"

Silence envelops the room. Even the transforming lingo-spot doesn't try to fill it. Somehow, it understands that the silence is the very thing being said.

"Sally, my wife and four of my children are dead. Of my original family, only two daughters have survived. I do not need to be reminded of what things in life are authentic, and which are passing distractions. I do *not* need to be lectured on whether I am in some kind of flight—"

—from grief.

Jefferson doesn't finish his sentence. But I know. He pauses again, and smoothes out his long coat.

"I am sorry, Sally."

"I'm sorry, too, Tom."

"You really shouldn't call me Tom." Jefferson turns back to me and puts his hand on the leather box next to the excavated bones.

He flips the box open, and I see Eli's cap inside.

"I need to know how this fits into the puzzle. I need to know what the link is between you and the boy and the lizard man. I need to understand if there is an immediate danger confronting us. I am beginning to suspect that you are not this 'Brassy' who belongs to Governor Claiborne. But I'd like to know who else you might be."

I don't know enough about the history of Eli's country—the United State, I believe it's called—to know what is supposed to happen next in the years between the presiding of Jefferson and the invention of time displacement by Eli's parents. I do not how things turn out—if there are wars or not, whether the slaves stage a rebellion, and whether the leaders of this United State are always wise and just.

I do not know; but if I did, it wouldn't matter.

It would appear that because Eli, K'lion, and I have been loosed upon history, history itself is no longer quite fixed. Or to put it another way, since we can now travel into the past, the past therefore becomes as unpredictable . . . as the future.

"I am taking this cap with me to Washington tomorrow. I wish Ben Franklin were still here to look at it, to offer us theories about its electric properties. But I intend to have it examined, so its true nature may be discovered." The look on his face softens. "I wish you no harm. No harm at all, Miss Whoever-You-Are. But what else is *incognitum* in America that I'm not being told about?"

Sally watches Jefferson and me. She's waiting for an answer, too.

It never comes.

The door to the study bursts open, and Honoré is there with Patsy. They're having an argument.

"Sir! *Monsieur! S'il vous plaît!* Will you tell your daughter that macaroni and cheese do not belong together! That you regret having ever asked me to combine—"

"Father, I'm sorry for the interruption. I asked Honoré to make the dish the children are so fond of."

"Honoré—Patsy and I felt that putting macaroni and cheese together makes a simple, satisfactory American dish, and I would ask that you keep experimenting with the different cheeses to find the best possible combination. Any dish that all of my grandchildren like equally well without complaint should command our respect. Now, is there some other reason you have chosen to violate the strict edicts about my not being interr—"

But the word *interrupted* is itself interrupted.

I have reached into the leather box and pulled out Eli's cap. I can feel the tingle in my hands already.

There's no other way. If the cap disappears, so does Eli's ability to move through time with it. None of us might ever get back.

We would be stuck here, unmaking history.

"What—"

"I'm sorry," I say, as Jefferson lunges for me.

As he fades from view, the world around me

goes gray, then blue, then explodes in a frenzy of color, fog, and light.

If this is the Fifth Dimension now, it's different.

Or maybe I am.

And then I realize, I have no idea where I'm headed.

Chapter Thirteen

Eli: Fort Mandan
December 1804

There's one hour of warmth today—and I want to use it all. Of course "warmth" means anything less than about a million degrees below zero. It's anything that lets you step outside for a few minutes without worrying that if your finger touches your cheek, it'll be frozen there.

Not that your finger actually can touch your cheek, because cheeks and faces are bundled up in strips of cloth, and hands are usually wrapped up in these big smelly leather gloves that remind me more of baseball mitts.

I look like one of the zombie characters in a Barnstormers game now. Like a bundle of old clothes that suddenly came to life.

But which life? I really don't want to think about Barnstormers, or anything that reminds me of how *my* life was before.

Round and round our little fort I go, walking to keep warm, to keep distracted.

Since I've become tangled up in time, this place, this journey—this "now"—is the longest I've stayed in one spot. Or time. It's been half a year now, traveling with the Corps of Discovery.

I cover myself with stinky buffalo hides. I eat meat and jerky and nuts and fish. And I live with a bunch of guys who think that if I took a sip of whiskey every once in a while, it might help my growth.

They're good men, and they're brave, pretty much. Sometimes they're silly and weird. But I don't know how much longer I can keep traveling with them.

I have to find Clyne soon, and then we have to find Thea, and *then* we all have to get back home, to 2019, and get all this bad history sorted out.

I have an orange that I'm holding, deep in my pocket. It might be an orange freeze by now, but I know someone who'd like it, no matter what.

I had to trade my Christmas portion of brandy to get it, so it was well worth it. Lewis was handing out some fruits earlier that Jefferson had sent upriver for a special occasion. He had originally handed the orange to Cruzatte.

"Another of Jefferson's crop experiments evidently," Lewis said, trying to figure out what it was.

"A crop experiment will not inspire za muse!" Cruzatte said indignantly. So he was only too happy to trade.

I'd like to go across the frozen river to Mandan Village and show this orange to the shaman I keep hearing rumors about. North Wind, I think his name is. He's the one who is supposed to have seen the same "lizard god" that the fur trader Banglees saw.

But I can't just leave by myself, without permission from one of the captains. I've seen 'em actually whip guys for stuff like sneaking off.

So I keep tromping through the ice and blistery

winds, somewhere in the Dakotas, trying not to get distracted by the two things I'd normally be thinking about today.

"Merry Christmas, Eli! Want to play some baseball?"

It's Gassy. He's eating some of the dried apples that Lewis passed out earlier for Christmas presents. He also had a few big sips of the brandy that was part of Christmas breakfast.

The apples had been in the crates with other treats and were meant to celebrate both the holiday and the fact that we finished building the last part of "Fort Mandan" yesterday.

The fort is really just a group of small wooden huts surrounded by a big fence, right across the frozen river from the Mandan village.

You can see the round huts from here.

Lewis said the Mandan village is "the last known stop on the white man's map. Fur traders come up here. West of this, *terra incognito.*"

I've been meaning to ask him what that means. Maybe he meant "terror"? Like he's afraid of what lies ahead?

The Mandans and their neighbors, the Hidatsas, have been really friendly to us. They've sent food, and visited us, and had us over to the village for feasts. They don't celebrate Christmas, though.

Gassy's still waiting for an answer. The men all seem intrigued by "base," as they originally called it, until I updated them, since it was the game that helped get us out of that jam downriver. I left Kentuck's Fives ball with the Lakotas, but I've managed to make another one out of some old rags, and that's been usable. Barely.

"I can't right now, Gassy. I'm busy."

"Busy? On a field of ice on Christmas Day? The fort's built. There's nothing to do but freeze. And play. Oh, and fire off the cannon, tonight."

He's grinning when he says it. He's weaving a little bit.

"I know, Gassy. I'll be there for the cannon firing." I mean, that sounds cool, as long as it's not actually aimed at anybody.

He holds up the rag bundle and the small willow branch I helped carve into a vague Louisville Slugger shape.

"Come on, Eli. You can hit first. Christmas present."

Every mention of Christmas gets my thoughts all churning up again. It's not Gassy's fault. The last Christmas I spent was with my mom, in San Francisco, during World War II. And that involved keeping her from getting blown up.

I don't know what's happened to her since.

I don't even think it's been a full year since that Christmas happened. Not for me. That's another problem with time travel. Holidays don't obey any rules about how often they're supposed to come.

That might be good if, say, you really liked Halloween, or chocolate Easter eggs. But not when you're missing somebody on Christmas.

I miss my family. And if I find Clyne, maybe I can get back to them.

"Sorry, Gassy. I don't think I feel like it right now. I don't feel very Christmasy."

"But you feel cold, don't you? That's Christmasy. And you said you love this game. Besides, what else is there to do?"

I don't know. Maybe he's right. Maybe that would cheer me up.

"Eli will be coming with me." Lewis had come

out of the fort, wrapped up like some shaggy swamp creature from a Comnet cartoon, like the rest of us. "I know it's a holiday, but I've got to walk across the river to the village and see about hiring that French trader who came into camp. We could use him as a guide for the second half of our journey."

"That Charbonneau fellow they were talking about around the fire the other night? You want him to be our guide? Sir?" Gassy asks.

"Well, I'm actually more interested in hiring his wife. She's not much older than Eli here. Her name's Sacagawea. She's supposed to be a full-blooded Shoshone, and we'll be meeting that tribe sometime in the spring. She may know the area, and we could use a translator."

"Well, that's too bad the pair of you have such highfalutin important business on Christmas Day," Gassy says. "Forgettin' already it's a holiday and such. But you both have yourselves a good time with the Mandans." Still grinning, he throws up the rag bundle, swings the branch, and knocks a pretty good pop fly out over the snow.

"You don't mind the walk, young squire?" Lewis asks me, after Gassy goes after the rag ball.

"It's best to keep moving in weather like this, sir."

As we walk across the ice toward the village, I lose my balance and almost drop the orange. Drawing closer, we can smell the sharp smoke trailing from the chimney-holes on top of the round huts.

"You seem to be feeling particularly alone today, Master Sands," Lewis says at last. The words are muffled, and he has to say them more loudly than usual, in order to get them past all the fur strips. "Missing anyone in particular? Anything or anyplace?"

"Nothing—no one—that would make any sense, sir."

"It never does."

Lewis lets the conversation stop there. We cross from the slick river ice to the mushier snow on the banks, which is a little easier to walk on. Lewis taps me and points to the largest of the huts. We walk toward it and pull back the flaps.

"Hello!" Lewis says. "Happy Holiday."

One of the Mandan men jumps up and begins shouting at us. I think we startled them. They were all planning on spending a cold day around the fire, and here we are, yelling about a holiday on a calendar they don't even follow.

The Mandan children surround Lewis and me. A couple of them touch me, giggle, then run back toward the fire and smoke and the grownups, in the middle of the lodge. All of us in the Corps still seem so strange to them.

We're the outsiders, with the weird customs. We're like Barnstormer teams, showing up in a new town. Needing to prove ourselves to everybody. To prove we can be trusted. Of course, in Barnstormers, it never works out.

Closer by the fire, I think I see at least one of the people Lewis had come for: Sacagawea. She's young—I mean, not as young as me, but she's still a teenager. With long black hair, tied in several rings down her back. And she's pregnant.

I walk with Lewis in her direction, when someone taps me on my shoulder and says, "You are probably looking for me." I turn to see another young Indian, about the same age as Sacagawea, who steps forward from the haze. He has a large painted blanket wrapped around himself. There are wolves on it. There are also stars, and what appears to be a planet, sort of Earth-like, except with two suns.

He motions for me to head back to the corner — well, the "round," maybe, since technically there aren't any corners — with him.

"I'm looking for" — I have to struggle to remember the name — "North Wind Goes," I say. "The medicine man."

The Indian nods. "He may have medicine. Or he may not. But 'medicine man' is a white term."

Did I say something wrong? I know that *medicine* can also mean "power," but I wonder if I've offended him. Hey, wait. He understood everything I just said in English. How could he? Unless . . .

"My name is now North Wind *Comes*. It's changed. I've gone out and come back."

Come back from *where*? I want to ask. Instead, it comes out like this: "I hear you might know the lizard man."

"The lizard man is just a rumor."

I hold out the orange.

"If you know this rumor, if you see him, would you give this to him? From me. That's all."

North Wind takes the orange in his hand and holds it to his nose. Then he looks into my eyes and nods.

"Then you must be Eli."

Chapter Fourteen

Thea: The Sklaan Room

February 2020

I watch Eli's father for several minutes, walking around the room. He's holding something in his hand: two prongs with an arc and a ball of light dancing between them. The light changes color, turning bluer and bluer as he comes closer.

He wears some kind of messenger bag at his side.

This room hasn't been lived in for a very long time. There's dust, and clutter, and the furnishings seem strange even by the standards of Eli's era, as though they're not quite of the same period.

Near me, on a shelf, is a brown glass bottle with an orange covering. The covering says OVAL-TINE, and I try to pronounce the strange word.

No sound comes out.

Eli's father hasn't noticed me yet, either. I don't want to startle him, but I need to make my presence known.

The blue light glows brighter still as he turns the apparatus toward me.

I try to speak, but still nothing. I reach for the Ovaltine jar but cannot grasp it. My hand goes through it, like a specter, a phantom. And I realize that as I hold my hand in front of the bottle, I can see both my hand and the glass container behind it. I am in the same ephemeral state as the projected light of Mother's in the lighthouse. I am here. But not completely.

What does this mean? What happened to me after I put on Eli's cap in Jefferson President's house? How is it that I am *mostly* here . . . but not quite?

Eli's soft helmet, the one he uses for personal time displacement, seems to have affected me in a different way.

Eli's father is staring at me now. The apparatus in his hand is a brilliant blue.

He's staring at me, but he doesn't see me.

Instead, he sets the portable down on the floor, where it continues to glow. Looking toward me, but not seeing, he reaches into his pocket and puts on a glove. And then another. Then he reaches into the bag and pulls out . . . a cloth of some kind. A . . . *sklaan.* The *sklaan.* The artificial skin covering I was given on Saurius Prime to keep me warm or cold, as needed.

I had given it away to a woman named Hannah, a refugee from Peenemünde. She was fleeing the slave caves of the Reich, where captives worked on building rockets that would be used to destroy more lives. That was the place that taught me just how fearsome the future could be.

What is the *sklaan* doing here?

"Sandusky . . ."

I say his name. I mouth it. Still no sound.

He looks at me, where I . . . where I'm not

standing. I'm floating. My feet aren't touching anything solid, either. It's like being in a dream.

But Eli's father keeps looking in my direction, with an intense, yet quizzical, look on his face. I remember those sorts of expressions on my mother's face. And in remembering, might cry damp tears if I were more solid.

Sandusky reaches into the bag and pulls out a small sharp blade. He begins to cut a piece off of the *sklaan*. Then he stands back and throws the cutting into the middle of the blue orb, like tossing meat onto a fire.

The blue light explodes.

I am surrounded by arcing, sparking streaks of lightning and other light that moves like liquid waves. It's as if a great sluice gate of water has been flung open, and I'm cascading into the middle of the room.

Sandusky, surprised, is knocked back into the shelves by the reaction. He turns to where I am, where the light is most intense.

"Thea?"

Now he can see me.

I try to speak. *Still* nothing. I nod instead.

"What are you . . . ?"

He steps toward me, stands in front of me, reaches out . . . and his fingers go right through me.

"Are you . . . are you . . . are you all right?"

I nod. Though how can I be sure?

"Are you a ghost?" He looks around, as if he might want to retract that question.

I shake my head no.

But then again, how can I tell?

"Where's Eli?" He's staring at my hair when he says it . . . *at the hat.* Even in an ephemeral state like this, Eli's cap is visible on my head.

He returns his gaze to my eyes. "Where are you now?"

That's a good question. Since I am not *fully* here, is part of me somewhere else? Has some of my life force been lost, perhaps forever, in transit through the Fifth Dimension? Am I also appearing as a ghost in Thomas Jefferson's Monticello at this same instant?

But I can't ask any of these questions. Not out loud. So, instead, I shrug.

Mother always hated shrugs. She preferred a good *no* to a shrug, even if she was looking for a *yes.* She loathed anything noncommittal.

"Is Eli all right?" A yes-and-no question. I could nod, if I knew the answer. But I don't want to shrug again. For Eli's father, that would be as bad as a *no.* So I nod. It's not quite a lie. It's giving us all the benefit of the doubt.

"Have you seen my wife?"

I shake my head. It's the first clear answer I can give him, and it's sad news.

"The dinosaur boy?"

His voice is rising. He has to compete with the sparking blue energy swirling around the room.

I'm so sorry I can't tell him what he wants to hear.

I'm so sorry.

I reach out for him.

He reaches back.

Our fingers nearly touch. But more sparks, not just blue ones, burn and crack between them.

Sandusky snaps his hand back. "Thea! What have I done to you?"

BOOM! BOOM! BOOM!

I can't tell him it's not his fault. Even if I could speak, he wouldn't hear me over the sudden loud thudding as the door flies open—*SHZZZT!*—and slams shut. I've seen this man before. He once ordered soldiers to open fire on a Saurian time-craft I was in.

"Hello, Sandusky."

He's there with a woman.

"Howe. Thirty."

There are two armed guardians behind them now. He's keeping the same kind of company.

Thirty—I wonder if she's a mathematician—and Howe both squint against the brightness.

"Quite a dramatic meeting, Mr. Sands," Thirty tells him. "And quite clever. We thought you had run away. And yet here you were, under our noses, in the most restricted area of the tunnels."

"Everything seems to be here. Every last splinter and crumb from the hotel room. Everything but my wife."

"She's never been here, Sands." The one

named Howe seems always impatient, whereas Thirty acts more like this is a game. "If you'd cooperate, maybe we could find her."

"And look"—Thirty makes her next move—"you've brought the artifact." She points to the *sklaan*. "We've kept that under very tight security, since our predecessors found it. You've been quite busy, Sands, stealing it, breaking in here, and contaminating the entire room."

"How long has this project been going on? How many 'Danger Boys' have there been before my son?"

It's not a game to Sandusky. But there's still some strategy. He has put himself between me—the apparition of me—and the intruders.

"Your wife doesn't appear here, Sands. She doesn't haunt this place like a ghost. We need you back in your lab. Helping us. Helping your country. Helping the *world*."

"You've taken my family from me. How much more help can I give?"

Howe doesn't respond to that but keeps looking around the room. Perhaps after you've done certain things to someone, it becomes impossible to look them right in the eye.

But Sandusky looks at Howe. "You even took a hotel room my wife lived in once and rebuilt it *here*, in this tunnel, where no one could find it. *Why?*"

"Things in the world . . . are not as under control as we would like, Sands." The guardians are moving slowly toward Eli's father. Howe keeps talking to him. "It's dangerous for all of us."

"This isn't a man who worries about danger, Mr. Howe." Thirty still seems to be enjoying this situation. "This is a man who brings an alien artifact like that"—she nods at the *sklaan*—"into a room like this, hoping all the time-particle residue will ignite a reaction with his portable time-sphere. He wants to tear open another hole in time and space. This isn't a man who worries about danger at all."

"Maybe this is a man who needs to be left alone to experiment, if you ever want me to help you."

The guardians are steps away from Eli's father, but at these words, even Thirty and Howe involuntarily step forward. As everyone closes in, Sandusky is forced to adjust position and can no longer block their view of me.

"My God." Howe stares.

Thirty moves toward me. I move — drift — aside. She circles around me, then looks at Eli's father. "So, Sands, do you know this . . . emanation?"

He doesn't answer.

"We've seen her before, I believe." She motions at the guardians, who lower their weapons, pointing them at both Sandusky — and Mr. Howe.

"This room is contaminated in all sorts of interesting ways. Mr. Howe and Sandusky, you'll have to stay here. And so will the girl. However much of her there is."

Howe seems shocked. "But —"

Eli's father just shakes his head. And laughs.

Thirty continues. "We'll say it was slow pox and keep these corridors sealed off."

The laugh turns into a sudden roar as Sandusky charges Thirty. "Taken . . . *everything*!" The guardians look like they want to fire, but Mr. Howe, still loyal to her, tries to stop his charge, and they don't have clear aim.

As Howe and Sandusky grapple, Howe is spun toward the center of the room, toward the *sklaan,* and the glowing blue orb. Toward me.

Howe hits me first.

But there is no "hit," no impact, just tingling, and the skittish release of even more energy.

Howe flails his arms and tries to grab ahold of me, to slow himself, but I'm not solid.

And then it starts to feel like there's an electrical storm, like it did when Eli and K'lion and I were ejected from the Saurian time-ship and fell through the Fifth Dimension, seemingly so long ago. . . .

From somewhere comes the sound of one of the guardian's weapons firing.

Howe still tumbles, still trying to hold me, but he can't. I'm not really all there, all here—I haven't been all *anywhere* for a while—but still, he slows down going through me. It's as if I am made of sticky ether. Then he slips away, and much to my surprise, it feels like he's pushing me along with him, like we're tangled up. . . .

There are more flashing lights and then *BAM!*

I hit something really solid. Somebody falls on me, or over me, and knocks the wind out of my stomach. There are screams and running feet, and then I hear a voice. Sally's.

"Amazing, child. We thought we'd lost you for good."

Chapter Fifteen

Eli: Sacagawea

February 1805

Thwap!

The bundle of rags lands in the snow. Well, of course it lands in the snow. There hasn't been anything else for it to land in for months. And it's far enough away that I think we can count it as extra bases and say that North Wind Comes has a couple of RBIs.

It's my first time back outside since Sacagawea and the others found me. I had to promise both Clark and Lewis that I wouldn't run away and wouldn't go looking for Clyne, "the big rumored lizard," as Lewis called him, on my own.

I promised. And besides, I just barely escaped getting frostbite the last time. I'm still thawing out, still a little sore. And it won't do Clyne or me any good if I get lost again.

Still, the two captains make sure there's always somebody around to watch me.

Right now, it's Gassy, watching the baseball game unfold.

He just told me that Sacagawea was inside the fort, having her baby. He heard the labor might have started a little early because she was outside in the cold so long, helping to find me. My hands go around the small jagged crystal she gave me, the one for good luck.

"Eli . . . I score?"

"A double," I tell him, and hold up a couple of fingers.

North Wind's English has gotten better in the three months we've been here. He's picked up a lot from me and the other Corps members.

It's better for both of us if he uses his English, rather than us being seen in high-speed Mandan/

English exchanges that might raise a few eye-brows.

But even though he has a lingo-spot—he must—he still won't tell me much about Clyne. A good shaman doesn't reveal many secrets, I guess.

Including the secret of where Clyne has been spending the winter. I think, with the harsh climate, North Wind's only been out to see him once or twice since we got here, anyway.

Once was to give Clyne the orange.

That was when I tried to follow him and it didn't work out so well. And it doesn't look like I'll get another chance to do that.

"What did you think you were doing?" Lewis asked me after that first time, when he felt I was defrosted enough to answer a couple of questions.

"I—I . . ." I stammered a bit, then fell back on the classic you use with your parents, when you tell one of them that the other said something was okay. "Jefferson. Instructions . . . from Jefferson."

Lewis shook his head. "I am dubious that your instructions included freezing to death in the Dakotas. In fact, I believe I am supposed to send you back in decidedly nonfrozen condition when the spring comes. Besides, a president shouldn't keep secrets," he added. "It's bad for the country. Even if the rest of us"—and here he looked right at me—"walk around with secrets all the time."

Did he mean my secrets? Or did Lewis have a bunch of his own?

North Wind came into the fort after my rescue to see how I was doing. "I have a message from your friend," he told me. "'Prolific thanks. And soon, a good time to meet.'"

A good time to meet. Clyne's favorite greeting. But this time, did he mean we'd actually be seeing each other?

Clark was nearby and overheard. "Does Master Sands have another meeting planned with the Indians? So soon? You've barely warmed up from the last attempt. Unless it means we're wasting money hiring Charbonneau and Sacagawea. Perhaps fate has already selected the translator's role for you."

It reminded me of something Thea told me

once, when we were in Clyne's time-ship. She got it from her mother, Hypatia: "The journey selects *us*, Eli. It calls us to it. Because, somehow, we fit the task."

I think Thea was trying to make herself feel better, since any thought of her mom usually made her sad.

But if the journey really picks us, instead of the other way around, then I do have to get to Clyne soon—not so he could be shipped back as some kind of specimen for President Jefferson—but so he and I can leave and find Thea.

So Clark should let Sacagawea keep her job, baby or not.

And that baby, it seems, is due any moment.

Lewis is with her, with his medical bag, along with some of the Mandans. LeBorgne, the Hidatsa chief, is in there, too. Since Sacagawea was captured by the Hidatsas, before Charbonneau married her, I guess he felt like he had the right to watch over things.

According to North Wind, LeBorgne's been in a bad mood ever since his favorite warrior, Crow's Eye, ran off.

That's why North Wind isn't in there helping out. LeBorgne has some kind of personal grudge against him because of the whole Crow's Eye thing.

But despite all those people in the room, or maybe because of it, the birth wasn't going smoothly. That's what we heard each time Cruzatte or York or somebody ran out to find some more firewood to boil water, or old cloth to use for towels.

"I shouldn't let LeBorgne keep me out," North Wind said, as we paused our game of over-the-line to watch another firewood run.

"Do shamans help deliver babies?"

"Shamans just try to improve the odds for everyone." He gave me a smile that seemed at least a few years older than he was. "Maybe even you."

He sounded like Lewis, who was always wondering about "the real odds of any of this succeeding—this entire elaborate journey."

Now Clark has come out. They sure must be using a lot of firewood in there.

He sees me and tromps over as fast as he can

in the snow. The look on his face isn't a happy one. "The baby's tangled. The baby's not coming." He looks at North Wind. "Sacagawea wants you. She insists. Lewis will handle LeBorgne."

North Wind doesn't reply right away, and in his panic, Clark turns to me. "Does he understand me?"

"He understands you."

"She's saying something about how North Wind Comes can speak with the animals, but she's feverish, so we can't be sure."

Since nobody tells me not to, I follow them inside the fort, where the constant smell of smoke and grease and sweat is mixed with something else.

There are voices, Mandan, Hidatsa, American, coming from the next room. I step in there, and when my eyes adjust to the firelight I realize I'm still holding the stick bat and rag ball I was playing with outside.

But it doesn't seem right to just set them down, even among the big mess of blankets and buffalo skins and pots of water and baskets of herbs and

Lewis's bottles of medicine. It doesn't seem right to treat it like just any room, because you can feel in the air that something serious, something special is going on here.

This is before I see Sacagawea.

She's on the other side, all bundled up, grabbing the hand of her husband, Charbonneau, who looks around like he wants a hand to grab, too. Amazingly, Lewis looks completely calm, kneeling next to her, dabbing a rag against her face.

She's resting on a pile of padding and hides, not lying down all the way, but not quite sitting up, either. There are some Hidatsa women behind her, helping to hold her.

Sacagawea's eyes usually sparkled if she looked in your direction, like she was really sizing you up in an intense way. Even half-frozen that day in the snow, I could feel the intensity in her gaze.

Now her eyes are glossed over, like all her concentration has gone inside.

And then she turns and one of the blankets falls away and there are her legs, spread wide open, and I've never seen anything like that, even on the Comnet when I looked at an image bank I wasn't supposed to go to. There's blood and goop and hair and a head. . . .

It's the top of a little head, but it's hard to see in the firelight. I'm squinting like crazy, but yes, I think it's the top of a head, peeking out from the middle of Sacagawea's . . .

. . . privates. There's more oozy stuff and a little of the baby's hair. It has really blue skin, which looks weird. How can a baby have blue skin?

I drop the bat and ball.

And then there's a loud groan, and Sacagawea slumps back, and I lose track of the head, and the baby's still not out. North Wind walks over to where Lewis is, but before he can speak to him, LeBorgne steps out from one of the corners of the room. I hadn't even seen him. He spins North Wind around.

"He's the one!" He points to North Wind for the benefit of everyone else, but Sacagawea just moans again. "Let him do some good now! He knows the lizard man! He will lead us!"

Lewis looks around, stands up, and wipes his hands.

North Wind isn't sure what's going on and calls me over.

"I thought I was to help," he says to me, low, in Mandan.

"He wants to help deliver the baby," I explain to Lewis. "He's the shaman."

"I *know* who he is," Lewis replies. "But the labor is becalmed. The baby may be tangled in the umbilical cord. Someone in here said that a rattlesnake's rattle, ground up and taken internally, might help the delivery. I never heard of such a use, but I'm willing to try it."

LeBorgne puts himself right in the middle of the conversation and switches into shout gear: "The lizard man kept Crow's Eye from becoming a warrior! He makes things happen that aren't supposed to happen! He's the one to get!"

I turn to Lewis. "So how come he wants the, um, 'lizard man' if what you really need is part of a rattlesnake?"

"It was LeBorgne's idea," Lewis says in a lowered voice. "At first he didn't want North

Wind in here, but as soon as he saw him, he switched the snake talk to bigger game and kept mentioning the lizard man."

"*He* should take us!" The Hidatsa chief points angrily at North Wind. Sacagawea keeps making loud noises. I bet an argument in the birth room is just about the last thing she needs right now, but she keeps a firm grip on Charbonneau's hand, which is a good thing, 'cause he looks like he's about to jump out of his skin.

And then I see the women taking Sacagawea and gently turning her over, so that she's up on all fours, on her hands and legs. She's trying to push the baby out from a different angle, and there's that blue head again, and everything else. I wonder if I'm blushing or if that's just the smoke and grease again. Who knew that a time-traveling baseball cap would lead to all this?

"Does anyone think the lizard man can help?" I turn to North Wind, mainly so I'll have some-thing—someone—else to look at.

"They think his skin can. LeBorgne convinced them that if a small rattler is good, a giant lizard is better."

"You mean—"

But LeBorgne answers the question for me: "With the lizard man's skin, the medicine between Hidatsa and Mandan will be made right again!"

"They want to kill him," North Wind tells me.

I look at him. "But they don't know where he is. Only you do. Right?"

North Wind doesn't speak.

"Right?"

But LeBorgne is full of answers. "And because we've had the shaman tracked, we know where that boy was heading!" He points at me. "We know the lizard man is hiding in the Spirit Mound! A new hunt calls to our wintering bones! Who is with me to save this baby and kill this wicked demigod?"

A cry goes up from a couple of the men near LeBorgne, who whoops back at them. The women in the room hiss back at him to be quiet, but he ignores them and charges out, the men following.

"What just happened?" Lewis asks me.

"I think I'm going back out there," I tell him. "I don't have a choice. And I definitely won't be alone." I turn to North Wind. "Are you coming with me?"

He nods.

"All this time, I was trying to protect him," North Wind says.

Sacagawea groans again. This isn't what she had in mind when she called for a shaman.

Chapter Sixteen

Clyne: Silver Throat

I've made contact with another mammal species here. Maybe I shouldn't give up yet on the idea of getting home and filing more extra-credit reports. Not because, in the entire grand Cacklaw field of life, my own grades are important, but because things are so routinely unpredictable here that Earth Orange—and mammal culture—continue to cast doubt on every established Saurian theory about the orderly progression of life, and the ultimate purpose of evolution.

The other species I'm now in communication with are called wolves. At least, that is how humans have named them, and it is these wolves who have been living in the Spirit Mound, in a kind of nest-community called a pack. Their tribal leader is a matriarch called Silver Throat.

I am on a hunt with them now and remain hopeful that soon I will see Eli.

After my seasons living with the pack and healing up, I am also hopeful that my lower limb will again experience full and true functionality.

They were wolf eyes that had surrounded us last winter in the dark.

"They have come to rescue their devil brother!" Crow's Eye shouted, looking into the orb-populated shadows of the Spirit Mound. I gathered this meant Crow's Eye had suddenly become a believer in the stories about this place. Trauma makes mammal minds very elastic. "Let us die bravely, North Wind! Let us give our tribes a new tale to tell in snow season!"

And then he had his knife against my throat.

"Why bother?" North Wind said, helpfully pushing the knife away from my throat. "They won't tell stories about a shaman who could not protect a god-spirit." He nodded toward all the visiting eyes. "And we still don't know what kinds of stories *they* tell."

Couldn't either of my human companions smell the deep woolly mammal scent that goes with the eyes that are peering at us? Would it be up to me to make an introduction?

"Shamans talk too much." The knife flashed back in my direction, and this time, North Wind couldn't stop it. I rolled out of the way, even with the jabberstick in my limb and the deep rumbus of pain in my leg. The blade just missed, and I started to wonder if I would have to bite Crow's Eye, or at least growl to scare him off. As ridiculous as mammals are, I've never had to hurt one. Yet.

"Crow's Eye—"

But North Wind didn't have a chance to finish.

The eyes began a long, low music together. A chorus. It reminded me of the Song of the

Gurdlanger, a song cycle chanted by the armored, horned Saurians who served as King Temm's guards, when the time came to bear his body away at last toward Saurius Prime's two falling suns.

Like those songs, the Spirit Mound music captured both a sense of timelessness, of the eternal, and the utter, fleeting swiftness with which all things pass. It was sweet and sad all at once.

The howling, growling sounds must have reminded North Wind and Crow's Eye of something, too. They stopped — Crow's Eye forgot all about his blade and making a story out of me — and looked with new appreciation at the eyes encircling us.

One pair of eyes stepped into the pool of flickering light. She was fur-covered, walking on four legs. Long snout, inquisitive, intelligent face.

At first, I thought she was a dog, but the spreading rumbus of pain in my limbs was wreaking havoc on my taxonomy skills. She and her companions were larger than dogs. A pair had been kept in the zoo in Alexandria, in Thea's time.

The one who stepped forward was silver gray,

a female — and a leader. You could read it in her bearing. She cocked her head at me, forming a question with no spoken language whatsoever. Her eyes were fierce and filled with green fire. They stayed locked on me when she spoke.

In the snow outside . . . we watched. You left a substance that allows us . . . to understand the humans. And you.

There was some of the lingo-spot left outside after my experiments! And it was on her now!

We could hear it . . . resonate. I tasted some.

She'd ingested infected slow pox! My laboratory methods were getting so sloppy I could be set back several grade levels if I ever made it back home.

"The substance you speak of . . . has become tainted, transformed," I said, overriding my self-aches to speak up, so North Wind might hear me, too. "I would advise strongly against ingesting any more."

It was a sad piece of advice to dispense on a planet so badly in need of good translation, like Earth Orange. I looked at North Wind.

"I should have told you sooner, but circumstances remained hopscotchy."

"Is the talking-substance dangerous to me, then?"

"I am hoping it is merely changed—but I need to do more research." The pain was getting the best of me. I wanted to make a few good notes before passing out. "So . . . what kind of mammal dances do you do?" I asked, not sure if that was the right first question to ask a new species.

The gray fur's eyes widened. She uncocked her head and I looked at her face. I read acceptance and the merest whiff of a deeply wise sense of humor there.

Dances? Some mammals we hunt and eat; others we ignore; some we play with; others, lately come here, wish us harm. Those two-leggeds—she nodded toward North Wind and Crow's Eye—*call us "wolves." My clan calls me Silver Throat.*

Another wolf with reddish fur came up and growled something to Silver Throat. She answered the red-fur with a soft series of growls, then turned back to me. *My daughter, Birdjumper. She tells me not to ingest any more creations of yours until you grow more sure of them. She reminds me to be wary. I need no such reminders. But what kind of two-leg are you? You look almost like a big fish.*

That was my introduction to Silver Throat. I drifted in and out of consciousness for a few days, and while North Wind grew to accept our multi-mammal situation, Crow's Eye did not.

Both of them eventually left the Spirit Mound, with the wolves' blessings and the wolves' guidance in finding hidden passages to take them out.

I remained, in order to heal. The wolves, for their part, would occasionally lick my wounds—especially after the jabberstick was removed with a searingly painful yank by Birdjumper—and Silver Throat and I would converse.

"Perhaps someday you could see my home, as well."

You mean, journey with you?

"Yes. You might be able to get a job teaching philosophy."

To humans? That might be difficult.

"To Saurians. You could come to Saurius Prime."

Where you fish-people live? But you say I wouldn't be allowed to hunt.

I loved talking to Silver Throat. Conversations with her kept me alert and ready for debate class. I enjoyed talking to North Wind Comes, of course, but I didn't see him as often. His people have placed confidence in him as a healer and now have more need of him.

And of course, there is Eli. After his gift of the orange, it was my wish to leap straight into the Mandan village to greet him quite loudly with maximum friendship.

But Silver Throat, and later North Wind, advised me that wouldn't be safe. Eli is traveling with an exploratory regiment that might wish to harm me out of pure reflexive action. North Wind doesn't feel his people are ready to have me show up in his village.

But when I heard Eli had come looking for me and nearly perished, I felt I must make contact with him soon. After all, we have to find the time-vessel and find out what effects mammal-borne disease is having on it. I fear ever greater chaos within the human time stream the longer we are delayed.

And so I have agreed to come on one of the wolf pack's winter hunts. To strengthen myself, to catch a glimpse of the village where Eli is, and formulate a *gra-baak*-proof plan to rendezvous.

If you join us on the hunt, Silver Throat said to me, *you can share the meat.*

If I start actively hunting mammals, I replied, *I will be in even greater violation of every Saurian agreement made since the end of the Bloody Tendon Wars. I've already been living off the meat you've provided. An even more severe appetite for flesh would create enormous social problems on my home world. And, furthermore, would be very bad manners here among my hosts.*

I had eaten bird bones when foraging on this planet, but I dared not pursue larger game. Especially involving my host phylum.

There is a stray, solitary ungulate ahead of us—an elk, I believe—separated from its herd. Silver Throat watches while members of her pack surround it. Soon she will join them to take down their prey.

Thankfully, the limp from the jabberstick keeps me from being a more effective hunter.

Did you not say that returning to this other home of yours is a matter of both distance . . . and time?

I nod.

But time only moves in a single direction. There's no going backward, no matter how much we wish it. That animal's life will end in a few moments. She nods toward the elk. *In its last moments, it will wish to undo its end. But none of us can undo endings. The stream takes us all.*

"That's why I need to find my ship. The stream may be flooding in all directions, if we're not careful."

A ship like the watercraft that humans use?

"More like the aircraft that they will come to use in their future."

The humans will be able to move around by air? That is very worrisome.

The hairs on the back of Silver Throat's neck have risen up, ever so slightly. But it doesn't seem to be caused by the consideration of airborne humans. Her nose twitches, then she springs to all four feet, growling.

Birdjumper and some of the others come running in from the outside. They're wet with snow and ice.

Birdjumper and her mother exchange yelps and growls. I can make out some of it, but not all. The humans are . . . moving?

They're coming right now. Silver Throat looks at me. *On foot and horse. The one you know is coming, too.*

You can see the figures moving toward us.

The wolves are sounding a retreat. And then I understand why: They aren't the only ones hunting today.

The humans are after *us*.

Arrak-du . . .

This won't be a friendly encounter. You can feel it.

And Eli's with them.

It's been so long since I've seen him.

Whose side will he be on?

Chapter Seventeen

Thea: Canal Street

February 1805

They've finally decided I'm well enough to travel. For months, I've been "rehabilitated" at Monticello, quarantined on Mulberry Row by Mr. Howard while Jefferson President was away at the capital.

My "fevers and fugues" were to be "sweated out of me" until I was "fit to be returned," in Mr. Howard's words, "in working condition."

So I spent my long days planting and gathering crops, spinning cloth, sewing, mending, washing, watching over the slave children and sometimes, if they were outside, Jefferson's own grandchildren.

I lived in a shed near Isaac's, with some straw on the floor, a couple of blankets, and two servings of food a day—stews made of greens and the cast-off parts of farm animals, like cows and chickens. Sometimes there is an allotment of a pasty substance called cornmeal. And once in a while, I have received a pudding made of something called a pumpkin.

But what matter my diet? Eli's soft helmet was gone, and I had no more visits or visions of the future. I kept looking for chances to escape, to somehow return to my friends.

There were none.

In spite of living near Isaac and the horse stables, I had no opportunities to be alone with the horse Sooysaa, either.

But I did see him on the day he was taken away.

Isaac held him by the reins and brought him down the row.

"Where is he go?" I asked, in the English I was using more and more.

"Where troubled horses go, little miss. Now you best move aside. Don't spook him."

Sooysaa reared up when Isaac spoke, and it took more slaves to subdue him.

I don't know where he was headed.

But my journey has been less mysterious. After my rehabilitation, and Jefferson President's return from Washington, I am being returned to my "owner," a man named Governor Claiborne— Claiborne Governor?—in a city named New Orleans, in a region called Louisiana. During a festival called Mardi Gras.

The festival has started already, and it is the reason I was given for the repeated explosions of light and large rumbles of thunder in the sky.

When the light flashes, I remember my journey through the dimensions and my visit to Eli's time.

Show . . .

There's been no one I could tell.

. . . *me.*

I've tried to talk to Sally about it but don't want to get her in trouble. Sometimes I feel like light is exploding inside me, too, looking for a way to come out.

Another boom fills the air. "That one's not a firework—that's from God." Sally turns to me, her face covered in feathers. "Maybe you attract lightning, too." She smiles to let me know it's a small joke, but around Monticello, Mr. Howard let it be known that I was "spooked." Sally wasn't allowed to spend much time alone with me, anyway.

We couldn't even ride down together in the same carriage. I was not outside, on the top, as I was that time with Sally. Instead, I was kept behind a locked carriage door, on a hard bench across from Mr. Howard, who watched me the whole time.

Even when we stopped to spend the night at various inns—or rather, when Jefferson did, since the slaves slept in barns—Mr. Howard seemed impervious to sleep. Whenever I'd awaken, he would still be watching me.

I could scarcely exchange words with Sally. At what point in the journey did she start wearing feathers?

"Sally . . ." I have so much I want to tell her, but so little English. Maybe now's the time to give her some of the lingo-spot.

Except then, would she wind up like Sooysaa? Like me? With the voices cascading in whether she wanted them to or not?

Even in the shadowy moonlight, my eyes do the job of my tongue. She sees me looking at her costume.

"Do you like it? It's for Mardi Gras." She turns around to let me see all of her cloth feathers. Facing me again, she raises the wooden beak off her nose, so I can see her more clearly in the dark. "I'm an American Eagle." Then she looks at me, trying to see what else can be read in my face.

"I know why they brought you back, Thea. Aren't they even going to let you wear a disguise? Just for tonight?"

I gather that costumes, or disguises, are required for this Mardi Gras — "fat" something, if my sense of the Latin is correct. But I have only the dress I was wearing at Monticello.

There is laughter as a group of people walk down the street near us. They have noisemakers and horns. One appears to be dressed like an insect; another, like a giant goat; and another, still, appears to be a type of fool or trickster, with a mask of exaggerated facial features and outlandish baggy clothes. The fool laughs. The insect seems to stare at me.

"They're headed to the river," Sally says. "You know, all those articles about you in the *Truth*, you've become famous. They even ran that portrait of you. You don't need anybody staring at you. Put this on." She hands me the wooden beak. She wants me to tie it around my face.

As I do, she explains how it is that I have become famous, perhaps even infamous, in the last few months.

"Brassy" sightings continued even after I was at Monticello. These caused Jefferson President a nearly endless string of political trouble, since Brassy was supposed to "belong" to Governor Claiborne and should have been returned right away. As president, Jefferson couldn't be perceived as taking the side of a slave in a runaway dispute, especially a slave who was, according to the rumors, getting ready to lead a slave revolt.

The rumors, and Jefferson's troubles, grew as

sightings of "Brassy" were reported in far-flung areas: in Virginia's own Alexandria; in the capital, Washington; down here in New Orleans. Each sighting of the "ghost slave" was then reported in something called the *Weekly Truth.*

"Jefferson hates that paper. Says he's not sure if Tom Paine is behind it or not, but it's always stirring up trouble."

I wonder if the random appearances of Brassy, or rather me, had to do with my travels through the Fifth Dimension? Could it be, with Eli's cap on, that I was somehow "split" in two? One self not fully appearing in the world of Eli's father while another kind of remnant emanation was left behind here?

Was I at risk of becoming a ghost?

"In any case, Jefferson's problems just kept piling up," Sally says. "He had to agree to come down here and give a speech—which he hates to do. To try and make it up to the governor, since it was his slave he lost. Mr. Howard keeps worrying that the situation isn't 'stable enough.' And you know what? It turns out, for once, that man may be right."

Evidently, Brassy had been seen recently in the New Orleans area, calling for a mass slave escape on Mardi Gras night. Carnival time. Or so claimed the *Weekly Truth*.

Consequently, there was a bounty hunter in the area, looking for Brassy. He was describing her to locals, saying she was dangerous, saying she might be seen in the company of "a white boy" and, according to the *Truth*, "other creatures too strange to mention."

"They decided to let all the Mardi Gras balls still go on, though," Sally explains to me, "to show they aren't afraid. Since the president had you all along, they want to make a big show of handing you back. Except they did add a curfew, so everyone would have to go home early. Those costumes you saw were headed to one of the parties: American, French, colored. They all celebrate separately. Only the Creoles seem to mix it up a little."

"Creoles?"

"Native Louisiana people. They're kind of like a big stew of different races already—Spanish, French, sometimes Indian or colored, all in the same blood."

"But Sally, it *is* the same blood. It's just *blood.*"

"I know that. And you know that. But when someone keeps slaves, I guess they have to pretend to *not* know that."

Brassy, or her ghost, evidently had called for using the parades and disguises to transport recently escaped slaves straight out of the city. They could march their way to freedom, under cover, I suppose. It was a good idea, except that somehow everybody had heard about it.

According to the paper.

That's why there are armed guardians patrolling the streets.

That's why Mr. Howard had me put in leg braces, sitting in the wagon, with strict orders for the guardians around me that I was to stay put until everything was ready for me to be handed over.

Sally looks around, to make sure no masked insects or armed guardians can hear us. "Since you couldn't come into Jefferson's house, you missed a real nervous visit from this governor. He's all worried 'cause a lot of slaves seem to be up and disappearing outside New Orleans and no one ever sees 'em again, anywhere. And the governor wants to put a stop to it. Jefferson felt forced to go along. 'Politics,' he called it. 'Sally,' he told me one time, 'it's politics that has me thinking the office of president might have already outlived its usefulness.'

"And then later that same visit, one of the governor's slaves whispered to me that it was magic helping the escapees. Magic that you could find right here in New Orleans, for a price. Maybe from one of the fortunetellers. I don't know if I believe it, but I told Jefferson I wanted to investigate this thing from the slave side, in case somethin' bad was happening to 'em.

"There were other reasons they couldn't shut down Mardi Gras. The French refused to be deprived of their celebration, the Americans refused to be shown up by the French, and the Creoles said they were free to do what they pleased. So, because we still have the masked balls and the parties, I have my disguise, and I think we should find out what's happening."

"Are you running away, too, Sally?"

"I'm too famous to run away, missy. I'm President Jefferson's favorite slave." She isn't saying it like she means it as an honor. "But I have to find out about this . . ."

Boom.

Show me.

There's more thunder, and another crack of light pierces the night, the way the light from Pharos used to with its great beam. Then I notice light from someplace else: under Sally's clothes, her costume, from her feathers. She takes out a small glass vial with a shifting, glowing mass contained inside.

I recognize the material. It's plasmechanical.

It's from K'lion's ship.

"The governor's slave, her name was Tomasina, gave this to me at Monticello, when nobody was looking."

Clop clop clop.

"These get passed on to the people fixin' to run away to freedom. Helps 'em find the trail, or something. Like a pathway, or one of those new railroad lines." She glances over her shoulders. "I got somethin' else, too, for when nobody is looking."

Revelers—I see the insect and the goat running in the opposite direction from which they came—are now fleeing up the street. Ahead is another small squad of guardians, armed with long weapons and dressed in their triangle-shaped hats.

The people in costume run ahead of the soldiers—*clop clop*—who stay in formation and move like a dreadnought, splitting the seas.

Sally is counting. "Three . . . two . . . one . . ."

And just as the guardians clop by, with people fleeing ahead of them, the men who watch me begin to fall out of formation to see what's happening. There is another roar of thunder—Sally keeps counting—and then another blaze of lightning, during which she moves her pretend feathers to cover up her own swift motion.

"Come on, child."

She unlocks the leg irons with a key that suddenly appears in her hand. The braces fall away and drop to the pavement. Then she grabs me and starts running.

"How did you —?"

"Slaves gotta keep their eyes open for each other, child."

"You, there! Halt!"

Two of the soldiers who had momentarily ventured into the boulevard now turn and come after us.

"Stop, I say!"

We're running in the direction the revelers came from. Ahead of us, I can see the canal — or I can at least smell and hear the water.

"Sally! You can't! You'll get in trouble!"

Tied up to one of the moorings near the water is a small boat. A man stands in it, nervously puffing a small clay pipe that produces smoke like a steady fire. Sally holds out the small vial to him. He nods quickly.

"Banglees?" Sally pants.

"C'est moi," the man agrees. "But I don' know if I want the trouble." He points toward the rushing soldiers and hurriedly unties the boat. "I may jus' celebrate this Mardi Gras by myself!"

"Wait!" I yell.

"*Pardonnez-moi,* but I cannot stay!"

"We need to know about this!" I hold up the plasmechanical orb in Sally's hand.

"I think after tonight, zat doorway ees going to be closed."

"What? What doorway?" I shout.

He has the last of the rope uncoiled from the post.

"Stay there and do not move, under the severest penalty of martial law!" the closest soldier yells.

"I told Jefferson I would do this on my own. Letting you go was my idea," Sally whispers. "I thought we could make it."

Boom!

Another firework.

Boom!

More thunder. But none of it distracts the soldiers this time.

Wait.

I might just be wrong about that.

That's not lightning. Or fireworks.

Zut alors!

The boatman has passed out. The soldiers have stopped clopping and are pointing their guns. Because those last two "booms" didn't just make noise and light.

They produced a boy . . .

. . . and a lizard man.

Chapter Eighteen

Eli: Departure

Clyne's locked up in a cage, and I'm celebrating in the Mandan village. Men dance around searing hot fires, wearing shaggy buffalo skins or hollowed out buffalo heads that cover their faces like big trick-or-treat masks.

But they're not dancing outside on a freezing cold night because they caught my friend. The dance is a buffalo-calling ritual, to tell the herds that it's time to start appearing again. I guess the winter meat supply is running low for the Indians. I know it's running low in the fort.

The dance is also the tribe's way of getting ready for spring. It reminds everyone that winter will eventually pass and it will be warm again. That's what North Wind Comes told me, the last time we talked.

When spring comes, I'm supposed to go downriver with Clyne and all the other "specimens" that Clark and Lewis are planning to ship back to St. Louis and, eventually, to Mr. Thomas Jefferson.

Clyne is the biggest specimen of all, of course. The plan is for him to spend the rest of the winter locked up, until we go. He'll be locked up while we're traveling and probably after that, too. Lewis is also sending a couple of the men back as guards, to make sure nothing happens to the shipment.

Until then, Clyne is supposed to stay inside his tiny wooden cage, right outside Fort Mandan, on the Corps of Discovery's side of the river.

He was out hunting with the wolves the day we found him.

"Hello, Clyne. How have you been?"

"Jabberstuck, but still inquisitive, and mostly well-hosted. There are things we need to speak of, though. A good time to meet, friend Eli!"

He might have talked more except that he was surrounded by spears and arrows and people who wanted to kill him. Especially LeBorgne. "You! You are the one who drove Crow's Eye away!" The man stood up and pointed to Clyne. "Kill this spirit! Kill him now!"

I stood in front of my friend, ready to protect him.

At that moment, I saw North Wind Comes. He jumped off his horse and ran toward me. You could see the breath leave his mouth and turn to icy steam as he moved.

"No, no! Do not listen to LeBorgne! Do nothing to the lizard man! You will bring terrible medicine on all of us if you do!"

The hunting party stood still a moment, looking at North Wind, at LeBorgne, at me, a little afraid of Clyne, and unsure what to do next.

Then we heard the crying.

One wolf stood over another, giving a long, mournful wail. There was an arrow sticking from the dead one's neck.

North Wind walked over to them. "Silver Throat. Forgive us for doing this to your daughter."

Then he turned to face the men again. "How stupid to kill a wolf for no good reason. Who did this?" But nobody said anything.

That seemed to be enough killing for one day, though. They decided to capture Clyne instead, and bring him back here. Where he remains in his cage.

But I don't think Clyne can last that long in such a tiny, enclosed space.

I wonder if he can see these bonfires from where he is? The flames are pretty bright. I don't know if it's the heat from the fire, but my lingospot seems to be itching like crazy. And I'm distracted, thinking of home, of Dad, and of Mom, wherever she is.

And Thea.

I try to let the music fill me for a couple of minutes, to slow down the swirl of thoughts in my head. There's drumming from the Mandans, fiddle music from Cruzatte, and lots of dancing around the flames, not only to call the buffalo, but also to celebrate the recent successful birth of Sacagawea's baby boy.

His name is Pomp. Or at least his nickname. I

think his real name is something pretty fancy, like John the Baptist. Or I guess the French version, which I think is Jean-Baptiste. Clark really likes the baby. Pomp was a name he came up with. And to everyone's surprise, Lewis doesn't seem to mind him, either. He even likes holding him.

Which is good, because Lewis was the very first person in the world to hold him. When we were out chasing Clyne, he found some powdered snake rattle in the fort's supplies. He gave it to Sacagawea, and it worked.

They didn't need dinosaur skin after all, and Pomp was born before we got back.

"Thinking about your lizard friend again?" I didn't even hear Lewis come up. He's holding a cup in his hand. "Some brandy? We're celebrating tonight. And hoping, eventually, to get fed."

"No thanks."

Lewis shrugs and takes a sip.

"We'll be leaving here, soon enough, and proceeding on. It's too bad you won't be joining us."

"I'll miss you, Captain. I'll miss everybody. They don't—" I searched for the right words. When I was a kid, I didn't worry about the right words so much. "They don't have many adventures like this left, where I come from. Not real ones."

"Where is it that you come from, lad? You've never really said."

"Like I said . . . the territories."

Lewis listens to Cruzatte's fiddling a couple more minutes, looking thoughtful.

"How is it, young squire, you came to be so expert in the ways of this lizard man? I didn't even believe the stories before. I thought Jefferson needed you out of his hair. Yet the beast is real, and you came to know him even before we arrived here. Do creatures like him live in your 'territories,' too?"

"I've . . . been on other expeditions with him," I say.

"And if I asked you what expeditions those were, I'd surmise you wouldn't answer."

"That's right."

"Presumably for my own protection."

"Yes."

There is a long silence between us then. The

music and drumming don't fill it. Both our minds are elsewhere.

"There is much we do not know, Master Sands."

I nod in the dark, even though he can barely see me.

"Perhaps there is much we should not know."

"I'm . . . I'm trying to get that part figured out, Captain."

"Like the president, and his *incognitum.*"

"What do you mean?"

"We are, all of us, always going about trying to name everything, trying to quantify it and understand it. I'm beginning to wonder if that's always the best idea."

"I still don't know what you're getting at."

"I'm wondering what will happen to your lizard man, your *incognitum,* once you and he are returned to Washington. You realize he will never be allowed to live freely, regardless of what or who he is?"

"I realize that, sir."

"I've seen you actually talking to him, when you thought no one was looking."

"Yes."

"Do you consider a caged specimen like that . . . a friend?"

"Yes, sir, I do."

The drums are getting faster, and Cruzatte tries to keep up on his fiddle. I'm stomping my feet on the ground, staying warm.

"This journey is teaching me about an otherness to things, Master Sands."

"I'm still not sure what you mean, Captain."

"An *otherness*. There is so much that exists outside ourselves, so much beyond our own experiences or viewpoints . . . so much *life*. It's as if our very bodies, as if every *thing*, were filled with an unknowable essence, an energy, buzzing all the time, like swarms of bees on the prairies we've just crossed, crashing against every other bit of energy in the universe, all making an incoherent whole. Sometimes all of existence overwhelms me, Master Sands."

I'm not sure, but he may have accidentally described the idea behind the reverse positron time-charge that my parents were working on.

"I've been overwhelmed a lot lately, too, sir."

"And sometimes I wonder if Captain Clark and myself are responsible for more than we realize. Like the very course of the future itself." He takes another sip from his cup. "For example, what will everyone think of their world once I send the lizard man back with you? Will they feel as safe as they once did?" He doesn't have an answer for himself. "You appear restless, young squire."

"I am, sir. I'm worried about the lizard man, too."

I stomp some more for my toes' benefit and listen to Pierre start up another fiddle tune. Some barking joins the music. "Ah," Lewis says. "Seaman is in a festive mood tonight, too. He's glad to be out of the fort, here with us, on this side of the river." There's another pause. "But perhaps you're thinking of going the other way, back to the fort, to see your serpentine friend." He sloshes the liquid around in his cup, like he's suddenly really interested in it. "While the rest of us are distracted here?"

What does he mean? Does he suspect something? "He's going crazy in that cage, sir. It's not good for his spirit."

"He's being guarded, you know."

"I know."

It seemed like Captain Lewis was trying to read my expression in the dark.

"These are all good men on this expedition, Master Sands. All good men. My wish for them is that none of them is harmed, in any way."

"That's a good wish, sir."

"I suppose that since we've been sent out to find so many things—new Indian tribes, water passages to the sea, tribes of giants—that it is unlikely we will find *all* of them."

"Probably not, Captain."

"Some of the things Jefferson expected us to come back with . . . may elude us, in the end."

"Yes." I think I'm getting what he's telling me. But I can't be sure.

"And perhaps, if we're not meant to know everything just yet about the mysteries of our lives and our times and our land . . . perhaps that's just as well. Perhaps that will leave room for other adventures later. Even in the territories you come from."

I nod. Of course, in the dark, I don't know if he sees me agreeing with him or not.

"All of which is a terrible thing for an expedition leader to say. So I expect I shall recant all this in the morning. But for now . . ." He finishes what's in his cup, then turns back to me. "But for now . . . Godspeed, young squire."

"Yes. Thank you, Captain Lewis."

"So you're walking back over the river now?"

"I'm not sure."

"I believe I shall be going back to the fire. I'm not always one for company, but tonight seems like a good night for it. Oh — take this." He reaches into his jacket and pulls out something wrapped in a heavy kind of cloth. He hands it to me. It's sort of slushy, like it's almost frozen. "What is it, sir?"

"A couple of servings of the portable soup I made. The paste. Wrapped well in oilskin. You need only add boiling water to it. In case you get hungry. Tonight, perhaps."

I take it and put it deep inside my coat. "Thank you, sir."

"You are welcome, young squire. And I will say it again: Godspeed."

And with the slightest tip of his hat, he walks away.

I wrap my buckskin jacket tight around me, put the soup packet between layers of clothes — though I'd like to avoid having to eat any of it if I can — and pull my floppy hat down as low as possible without blinding myself. I head out across the ice, back toward Fort Mandan. Back toward Clyne.

Using what moonlight there is, I walk carefully over the frozen river, long slow steps, careful not to land too hard, in case I hit a patch of thin ice.

Though there hasn't been much thin ice this winter.

I see a little flicker of firelight on the other side. Whoever had pulled guard duty at Clyne's cage was trying to stay warm, too.

I use the flames as a beacon, a kind of lighthouse, and keep walking toward them. I'm almost at the other side, ready to step up on the bank, when I hear a noise ahead of me. You can hear the whispery crunches on the snow ahead. Something's there, ahead of me. Waiting on the bank.

Something like a large dog. Seaman?

But it can't be. Seaman's on the village side of the river now.

And even in the little moonlight I have, I can tell. It's a wolf. Sitting there. Waiting.

Right according to plan.

Chapter Nineteen

Clyne: Reaction

February 1805

Evidently nothing went quite the way Eli had planned.

Being the true friend he is, he wanted to release me from the wooden cage, where once again I was to be specimen-probed.

Eli had arranged with North Wind to send the wolf leader, Silver Throat, to the fortification of the explorers, Clark and Lewis. She was going to bring the survivors of her pack and scare off the guards. This way, the guards would have a legitimate reason for leaving their posts and, perhaps, would not be whipped, as was the custom, for deserting them.

Such harsh penalties! Do mammals not take time to note the fragrance of their orange-graced world? If they did, it seems the consequences for small transgressions would necessarily be reduced.

Humans create such intrigues and problems for themselves. Eli's main current problem was that he would only have a short period of time to free me from this prison.

Silver Throat would then lead Eli and me away, back to the Spirit Mound, where we would meet with North Wind, who still hadn't returned to his people since Birdjumper's killing took place.

After resting, we would then follow Silver Throat's pack to another safehold, moving farther and farther away from settled human establishments. And when the spring came and rivers began to flow, we would navigate the waters again, on our own, and try to find Thea.

"Though you'd still be a big, giant scary lizard," Eli had observed, "to anyone who saw you."

That, anyway, was the plan. . . .

Silver Throat succeeded in scaring away the guards. She and her wolves swarmed out of the woods as if they were on a full-bore Cacklaw front press and ready for an actual attack. My watchers fled, presumably to get help, which would leave a few minutes for Eli and me to make our departure. But another human showed up before Eli did — or, rather, I should say, two humans: Sacagawea, a name with a regal high-Saurian elegance to it, and her hatchling.

"Pomp." Eli recognized the child. "Sacagawea, you shouldn't have come. It might not be safe — in a couple of minutes." My friend cast a nervous glance back across the river toward the mammal dancing.

Yes, finally, actual mammal dancing, and I, apparently, am to miss it.

"The baby was crying, and I was out walking with him, trying to soothe him. I saw the wolves come into camp. I thought you or North Wind might be here. And I wanted to say goodbye. To you. And the snake man."

"Actually," I informed her, "I am not related to the local snakes, but instead a Saurian —"

Before I could finish, she reached up through the bars and put a finger to my lips. "No matter which, I know you are a friend. And along with goodbye, I give you this."

She produced a small mineral sample. It was translucent, a crystal with a glow in its center from light that seemed to radiate from obscure parts of the spectrum.

"The flame stone," Eli said. "The one you used when you found me."

"Yes." Sacagawea nodded. "I would like you to have it for your journey."

"But it's yours. You said it's been with you since you were a child. Since you were kidnapped and sold."

"Yes. I always thought it might help lead me home. Now, with little Pomp here, I'm feeling that going home may be possible at last. So you take it now. You and the snake man need to go home, too."

Again, that flicker of thought: Where *was* my

home now? Was it my nest-source on Saurius Prime, or was it here, with my friends?

Some other light—firelight—moved on the other side of the river. This was a different kind of dance, the kind I had grown more familiar with.

"They've been alerted to the wolves now," Sacagawea said. "They'll be coming. Fare warmly," she said, rewrapping Pomp in the furry skins that humans permanently borrow from other animals. "Find good trails."

"And you"—Silver Throat looked at her— "guard every moment you have with your little one."

Sacagawea didn't have a lingo-spot, and I don't know if she understood the wolf, but before she was done covering her nestling, she kissed him. Then she waved at us and headed out across the ice.

"Wait—" Eli said.

She's delaying them, Silver Throat said. *For you. But hurry.*

The only trace left of her was her voice, giving song, drifting back from the dark ice:

Always riding out
Never coming home
The trail takes me far
Blood and honor
        dancing

She left singing of the *arrak-du.*

Eli regarded me. "All right. Then let's get that cage unlocked, Clyne."

"Yes. It is bound tight with strips of rendered skin."

"Leather."

"Yes. I had been steadily claw-tearing it when the guards were distracted. I will soon cut through the last of these practically applied tendons."

"Just hurry."

Eli warmed his hands with the mineral sample while looking over his shoulder. We both saw the portable firelights—*torches,* a word that's not quite as crisp as *taco* but is still interesting—on the far side of the river. The exploring party would soon be here.

"We have to pick up the supplies I left in the

woods. And we still have to get far enough to make it hard for them to track us."

"Friend Eli, may I see the flame stone in your hand?" While I worked on the task of freeing myself, I realized where I most recently saw light waves pitched to such arcane frequencies: Alexandria. They came from the light tower where Thea and her mother were doing their experiments.

Eli held up the small crystal. Even with only the nearby campfire and distant starlight available to refract through the prism, I recognized the glow. It's what my friend would call—

"WOMPER light."

"What? Clyne, what?"

The wolves growled. The torches were starting to make their way over to our side of the river.

"I believe a WOMPER particle is trapped in that crystal, orbiting inside a gas that may be trapped there from ancient times. There may be such stones on this planet. Thea's mother may have heard of their properties."

"Clyne, can you please get out of the cage? We have to go!"

"Oh. Yes, friend Eli. A good time for freeing."

I ceased work on the tendon straps that bound my cage shut. The jabberstick wound on my limb seemed to have healed, and I had just about enough room for a top-stompers Cacklaw move.

"Clyne—!"

"RRRKKKKGGGAAAHHHHRRRR!"

I hadn't roared like that since my playing field days on Saurius Prime.

The wooden cage shattered.

I was free.

The torches sped up.

"Hurry—"

Eli and I began a fast trudge over the freeze-blanketed surface. Silver Throat and her pack accompanied us.

"What I am saying, Eli, is that—in theory—if that is a WOMPER, and it could be freed and contained, we could catalyze a reaction, much like the time-spheres your sire created."

Soon the explorers would be at their encampment and discover our escape. My friend Eli would be in a state of severe reprimand consequence, on my behalf. There was no turning back for him.

"Can't you go any faster?" Silver Throat queried. Now that I was able to jump again, I probably could. But Eli could not.

"That, I think, is why the stone keeps you warm. The WOMPER creates a reaction at the core, winking instantaneously in and out of different time continuums. There is constant subatomic friction—"

"Clyne, don't you ever run out of breath?"

"But there is so much to talk about, friend Eli. Though all of this remains a theory, unless we can free the particle from the rock using a very high frequency."

We could hear the other humans behind us. They'd discovered our flight.

"High frequency?" Eli was talking to humor me, to distract himself. I could see the hard puffs of cold air coming from his mouth, even in the dark.

You mean a kind of song? Silver Throat asked.

"Right at the edge of human hearing. I don't know how to create it. And even then it would be what we called a 'wild,' or uncontained, reaction, with unpredictable results, especially because we'd have to use plasmechanics to contain the particle. The only such material is on the lingo-spots, and there is something I must tell you about the lingo-spots and everything else—"

"Clyne—"

"I regret not telling you sooner but there was no time—"

"Clyne—"

"Yes?"

"The wolves. Look."

Silver Throat had heard what I'd said about high frequencies. She'd gestured to her pack. They stopped and had begun singing, howling to the stars and the Earth's moon. They were making their own song cycle, with notes going higher, and higher still. . . .

A song of farewell . . .

Then Silver Throat joined the inchoate keening.

In the distance, the pursuing torches stopped.

Eli put his hands over his ears, after handing the flame stone to me.

I hurried, peeling some of the plasmechanical substance from my lingo-spot, from his, to cover the stone before it might crack, leaving just enough exposed to the direct sonic vibrations provided by our wolf friends.

What grand theory testing!

And now, in these long seconds, I wait, unsure if my field theory will prove true, or if we have just lost more time to our pursuers.

The song grows, and I am reminded once again of the song cycle of King Temm.

"Eli," I start to say—

—just as the WOMPER is freed and the wild reaction starts.

Chapter Twenty

Eli: Bayou St. John

February 1805

It feels like we've just been spit out by a thunder-clap, and I can tell from my stomach, and the swirl of lights we've been through, that we just moved through the Fifth Dimension.

We're in a city of some sort, by a small dock. It's nighttime, I see fireworks in the sky and light-ning on top of that, and we're surrounded.

Surrounded by more soldiers in *Nutcracker*-type clothes, by a couple of people in weird cos-tumes with animal heads, by a guy in a boat who's just fainted, by a woman standing in the boat—Sally, I think—who looked after me in Thomas Jefferson's tent so long ago—

—and by Thea.

Thea!

She calls my name—"Eli!"—and gives me a big hug, pulling me toward her. I now realize Clyne and I have appeared on the shores of the river, with our feet in the water, and I make a squishy sound as she hugs me.

"It's so good to see you!"

And then, just as quickly, she lets go of me. I don't know if she thought hugging me was too corny, or what. But I'm just as glad to see her.

"And it's good to see you, too, K'lion."

"A good time to meet, *ktk!* friend Thea," Clyne tells her, "and I am gratified to discover field-work with wild WOMPER reaction was *kng!* successful in drawing us here, doubtless *tkt!* due to a prime nexus."

"A what—?" I ask.

"Pulling us to this spot, together. A prime nexus is a crossroads of major outcome possibilities, first theorized in early Saurian time-venturing, and since borne out—"

Sally has been looking Clyne up and down. "I guess Jefferson is right. We don't know what's out there. But even though you can talk, lizard man, there's no time for that."

"You are right. I have to *tk-tk!* tell my friends what I now know about their lingo-spots *ssskk!* and the plasmechanical—"

"No, there's no *time* . . ."

The *Nutcracker* soldiers are snapping out of their surprise and rushing down the street toward the river.

One of the people in costume—he looks like a cat with an enormous head—comes up to Clyne and starts tugging at his chrono-suit. And then on his head.

"Hello!" Clyne says.

The soldiers stop briefly to watch. Until the cat person realizes Clyne isn't wearing a costume at all, and starts to scream.

Right after that, the soldiers started firing.

"Oh, lord," Sally says, jumping back into the boat.

Thea and I jump after her. It's another kind of pirogue, and Sally uses the long poles to push us along the waterway while the boatman is still passed out. When you're unstuck in time, hellos and goodbyes get constantly interrupted. I sort of said goodbye to Lewis, but not Gassy, Pierre, York, Clark, or even North Wind Comes. And I still haven't found out where we are, or where we're going.

It's like the Corps of Discovery all over again.

Meanwhile, there isn't room or time for Clyne to get in, so he's following us, jumping along on the riverbanks — or canal banks, since they seem to be more wall-like — keeping up with us.

"Does zat phantom 'ave to follow us here?" It's the boatman. He's waking up, pointing to Clyne, who hops alongside us, passing occasional small parades of people in costume who keep pointing to him like he ought to claim his prize somewhere.

"Yes, Banglees, apparently he does," Sally says.

Banglees! The name from Jefferson's camp. The fur trader who came back with the first reports of Clyne in the snow.

"Then I cannot take you wur I promised, because I will be trailing visions."

"Oh, you can take us. After all that's happened, I think we need to trust ourselves to the journey now. It'll tell us what it wants from us."

"Yes!" Clyne yells from the banks, clearing a low-hanging mossy tree branch that juts out over the water.

That Saurian hearing is pretty good.

"Sally *sskt!* may be right," Clyne bugles over to us. "We could all be drawn here because of prime *tkkt—tt!* nexus!"

"Prime what?" Thea asks.

"Nexus!" Clyne has to cut into the trees, due to the overgrowth, and we lose sight of him quickly in the dark. The canal goes through someplace called Bayou St. James, according to Banglees. The canal itself is a kind of packed-earth water road, a dug-out channel, but we're surrounded by swamp everywhere else.

Another flash of lightning gives us a quick electric snapshot of thick twisted oak trees, hanging moss, and tall grasses growing out of the water all around us.

"Nexus!" Clyne's back from his detour, and he jumps in the water, making a huge splash. Now

Thea's soaked, too, along with the formerly dry parts north of my feet. Even Sally and the bird-feather outfit she's wearing get wet.

"*Sacré bleu!*" Banglees yells. He grabs the long guide pole from Sally and is about to use it to thwack Clyne. "I am not frozen anymore! And you don't belong in New Orleans!"

"A good time to meet, *mon-ami* man! Can I not swim along?" Clyne asks. "Jumping ligaments still *ck-ck-ck!* sore. Swim muscles unused for many time clicks." He does a kind of sidestroke alongside us. "Feels both tumbly and nice."

While he swims, Clyne explains the "prime nexus" theory to us: In any universe, at any time, there are prime-nexus moments—like crossroads, where all history that follows is changed, no matter what.

"But doesn't everything we do affect history, no matter how small?" Sally asks.

"Yes, always—*sssh glgg!*" Clyne accidentally swallows some water in mid-agreement. He comes up, treading water, spouting the water back out of his mouth, like a living fountain. "Hmm.

Slightly brackish. But intriguing." Then he swims close to the boat again. "Think of it like rocks being thrown in this water. Different sizes make different splashes, different size circles. And some moments cast *skkkt!* bigger circles than others. The moments that change the most *tk tk!* things for the greatest number of life forms — those are prime *skw!* nexus moments. They have energy. They draw things toward *pt!* them. That may be why we are swimming in this dark *tk tk cht!* canal together."

"Um, Clyne," I tell him. "You're the only one who's swimming."

"I really had convinced myself it was an ice dream, from being frozen." Banglees shakes his head. *"Mon Dieu."*

Thea, Sally, and I get busy trying to figure out what the prime nexus might be. This trip has had so many of them: Lewis and Clark's whole journey, which changed all the history that came after, Thea meeting the president, even Jefferson digging up bones and discovering the past. All of it had an effect.

Has.

"What about him?" I point to Banglees. "Does he have anything to do with this?"

"I was not working for history," Banglees says to me, attempting to explain something. "I was working for money."

Banglees, Sally tells me, is involved in helping runaway slaves find something called "the doorway."

For a price.

"What's 'the doorway'?" I ask.

"That's what I want to find out. That's why we're headed to the lake."

"What lake?"

"Lake Pontchartrain," Banglees adds helpfully. "If we ever get there," he adds. Less helpfully.

"It ees very dangerous!" he says, to no one in particular. "Zat ees why I must charge!"

"What does this doorway do?"

"It makes people . . . disappear."

"Like my hat," I say. And then touch the top of my head. Why am I worried about getting to the lake? I'm still not sure how we're going to get back home.

"Sally — Ms. Hemings — when you were at Thomas Jefferson's, did you happen to see —"

"I lost your hat, Eli." It's Thea. Looking right at me with her big brown eyes. "I haven't had a chance to tell you everything yet. I lived in Jefferson's house, as a slave."

She's speaking low, in Greek, I think, letting the lingo-spot translate for her. Banglees is casually trying to listen in.

"What!?"

"I can tell you more, later. Your soft helmet — Jefferson had it. I tried it on, hoping we could all use it to go back. But then it was taken from me. I'm sorry." And now her eyes aren't looking at me at all.

My time-travel hat. With the Joe DiMaggio autograph. Gone.

"You . . . you wore it, Thea? Did you go back? What happened?"

Before she can tell me, Banglees spits out an urgent *shhhh!* and pulls the boat alongside another of the low, mossy branches.

"What is it?" Sally asks.

"A noise zat doesn't belong here. Shh. Shh."

There's a distant boom of thunder, but that's not what he means. There's the splash-splashing of Clyne, swimming up ahead.

"Cannot zat creature be si*lent*?" Banglees hisses. He's hearing something else.

"I don't know what happened, exactly," Thea whispers, continuing. "I went back for a little while . . . I saw your father."

"You did? Is he all right?"

"I'm not sure. He needs you. He needs your mother."

"How long were you there?"

"You people would make terrible trackers! *Shh!*" Banglees is getting more impatient. He ties up his boat to the branch and hops out. "Something ees following us." He walks along the bank of the canal, balancing himself, not making a sound.

He's pretty good. Almost like a wolf.

"Eli . . . I'm not even sure how long I was gone." Thea's still whispering. "But I've been back a long time. Worrying about you, and K'lion, for all the seasons we were separated."

She pauses suddenly, then says, "By the gods, Eli. I believe I've had . . . a nativity day."

"You've had a what?"

She tries it in English. "My native . . . day. Of borning. My day of borning."

"A birthday, child. She's telling you she's had a birthday." Sally was a better, quieter eavesdropper than Banglees.

"Happy birthday, Thea," I say. "How old are you?"

"Fourteen summers now."

Then I stop and realize I've been here for months, too. I've been traveling with the Corps. This is the longest I've been away since coming unstuck in time in the first place.

"Thea . . . I think I've had a birthday, too. Last August. Around the time Kentuck died."

"Who?"

"A friend. I wasn't even thinking about birthdays then. I guess I've had thirteen summers. I still haven't caught up with you."

"Happy . . . birthday . . . Eli." She sticks with English so I don't have to wait for the lingo-spot.

A bolt of lightning rips through the sky, and everything's a bright brilliant blue for a moment. Thea's looking at me like she doesn't know what to say next.

And then she leans over and kisses me.

It's a cheek kiss, mostly, sort of, I think. And it's fast. And I can feel a deep burning red wash over my face, all the way to the tips of my ears.

"I am glad K'lion is safe. And you, too," she says quickly. Still in English.

Sally is humming to herself. Her smile's just grown, and then she sees me looking at her, mostly because I'm not sure where else to look at the moment.

"Where is that man?" she asks, helping me to change the subject.

Boom. Thunder follows the lightning bolt.

"You!" I hear a voice shout, also in English.

"A good time to meet!" Clyne shouts back.

There's splashing, and what sounds like fighting—*"Zut alors!"*—and Sally doesn't waste any time. She grabs the guide pole, unties the rope, and pushes us into the canal toward the scuffle a few yards away.

"Who's there? Who's there?" Sally shouts.

It's dark, but there's just enough moonlight to recognize who Banglees is fighting with. It's Mr. Howe. And Banglees is about to cut him with a knife.

Chapter Twenty-one

Eli: Lake Pontchartrain

"Don't hurt him," I say to Banglees, nearly falling over as I step out of the boat.

"Why not? I think he ees a bounty hunter. He will turn us in." With his other arm, he has Mr. Howe in a grip by the neck.

"Why do you think that?"

"Because I use to be one! I know!"

I move closer. "No. I know him."

Banglees looks at me, looks at Howe, then releases him. He doesn't sheath the knife right away.

Howe tries to brush himself off. "What are *you* doing here?" I ask him.

His clothes are torn and muddy, and soon he gives up the idea of trying to clean himself off.

"Are you really here?" Howe asks. "Or is this some other part of the test?"

Back toward New Orleans, a lone rocket explodes in the sky.

"We are all really here. Some tracker." Banglees spits.

"You know who he is?" Sally asks, coming up behind me.

"I do."

"It feels like I've been here for months," Howe tells me. I squint at him. The dark covers him with shadows, but I can tell that besides being dirty, there are whiskers all over his face and he's lost weight.

"It looks like you have."

"Eli?" Thea's there when I turn. She's shivering, and not from the cold. "Eli . . . it's my fault. I did this. I brought him here."

"How?"

"When I was—when I had your soft helmet on. I was turned into a kind of ghost. I didn't fully . . . *materialize* . . . in your world. That's when I saw your father. That's when I saw *him*." She points to Howe.

"How did he get back here?"

"We were tangled up, fighting. He was caught in my . . . presence."

"You mean—you were a kind of time-sphere yourself?"

Thea nods, then shrugs. "I'm not sure. I felt someone with me when I was taken back here, as I moved through the dimensions. But I arrived alone."

"I have to ask Clyne if that's possible. If I—" I look around. No dinosaur. "Clyne?" And no answer. "Clyne?"

"I think he went on." Sally nods in the direction ahead of us.

"Are we close to this lake?"

"Uuuuuf!"

The question was for Banglees, who doesn't answer, because he's just been shoved by Mr.

Howe, who sprints past him, quickly disappearing in the dark.

"Come back 'ere!" Banglees yells, running after him.

"We've got to get to the lake," Sally insists. "We have to warn them."

"Warn who?" I ask.

"Any slaves there, trying to escape. Jefferson told me of the plans. Governor Claiborne's headed there, to find this 'doorway,' too. He wants to make an example of the slaves and end this runaway business. Jefferson may not be the most enlightened man, but he wants to prevent a massacre. Only, as president, he can't do it, officially. So it's up to me. And the two of you."

So we climb back into the boat, and Sally and Thea and I take turns with the pole, pushing and steering our way toward the lake.

And during my turn piloting the boat, I realize that in my months with the Corps, I've grown. My body's gotten bigger. My arms are stronger. I'm changing.

But then we get to the lake, and all the thoughts

about how long we've been here in this time, or how glad I am that Thea and Clyne and I are together, all those thoughts disappear in one huge thunderclap of surprise.

You'd think the surprise would be that the governor's troops were already there—a whole group of men, some of them soldiers, some who looked like farmers. Most of them brought rifles and fire. They brought dogs with them, too. Bloodhounds, I guess. Used for tracking.

And they had a bunch of people lined up, black people, sitting on their knees. They were all in costumes, or parts of costumes—wings and masks and papier-mâché animal heads—like they'd just come from a big party.

Didn't Sally say it was carnival time?

But none of this is fun; none of this is celebrating anything. They all have their hands behind their backs—men, women, children— and they're weeping.

You'd think all of that would be the biggest surprise, the biggest shock, but it isn't.

The biggest surprise of all is seeing Clyne's ship.

It's kind of wedged between two gnarled oak trees, pulsing, emitting a steady, low glow, and looking a little like — it's melting.

"The doorway," Sally says. "That must be it."

She means Clyne's ship.

"Nexus watch! Careful!" I hear Clyne but don't see him right away in all the shadows. Then a torch emerges from between the oak trees, near the ship. The light briefly touches on one of the dogs, who's digging furiously in the mud.

The light also shows Clyne, with chains on his wrist. He's being led by one of the soldiers, one of the guys in an actual uniform. He holds the torch up directly in front of Clyne's face.

"Get that costume off now, boy!" He tugs at Clyne's head.

"Ouch! Grab-twisting is not called for!"

"Don't talk to me. Don't try to fool me." Frustrated, the man turns away from Clyne and toward us. He seems familiar.

"Howard!" Thea gasps. "Jefferson's guard."

"Sure enough," Sally says. "It's Mr. Howard. I better get over there and talk sense to him before someone gets hurt really bad."

"No!" Thea says. In English.

"We have to keep him from doing something stupid to those people," Sally says.

Know.

"No what?" I ask. But I'm not sure if that was Thea or Sally. And my lingo-spot is itching like crazy.

"No," Thea says. "Not again. It's just like Tiberius." The gang of men, the torch light—it reminds her of what happened in Alexandria, to her and her mother. She's having that thing that people who've been through war get—a memory throwback. A flashback. Whatever it's called.

"No."

Know.

"No," I tell her again. "This is not like Alexandria. We'll be all right." I hold her. I don't want her to run and get hurt by the dogs. "It will be all right."

"It's always men with fire," she whispers to me.

"Yes," I agree. And soon we are surrounded, clamped into chains, and there's nowhere left to go.

Chapter Twenty-two

Clyne: Prime Nexus

February 1805

Perhaps it's too soon to think of abandoning my studies and becoming an Earth outlaw. We have found the prime nexus.

I am sure of it, and would love to pursue my thesis further.

The great turning point of history that may have drawn my ship here wasn't the journey of Eli's friends Clark and Lewis, or the death of Birdjumper, or anything else that transpired while we've been here, each of which, in its own way, will affect all history that flows afterward.

It wasn't even Steek's Theorem, which I was beginning to strongly suspect might explain everything: the loop-the-loop theory, from my home world, which postulates that by his or her very arrival, the time-traveler causes the upheaval in history—the disturbed time-wave—that draws that traveler or vessel to the prime nexus in the first place.

It's a good hypothesis, and Steek is a venerated scientist, but the prime nexus here has been found in bones and a medallion.

"A trail of American bones, each one yielding surprises." Jefferson, the clan, or nest, leader, whom Thea and Eli both already know, said that a few moments ago. He'd arrived in a wooden, wheeled conveyance—a carriage, I believe it is called—pulled by those four-legged mammals called horses.

Following Jefferson out of the conveyance was another man, dressed like a snake or serpent. Apparently, he had been attending festivities earlier in the evening, called Mardi Gras. I have yet to ascertain the reason for this festival. Perhaps the costumes indicate a human willingness to celebrate sharing their planet with other life forms.

The snake man took off his masquerade head, revealing a quite human head, with facial hair, underneath. He quickly let it be known he was a kind of nest leader, too—a "governor." Governor Claiborne.

An additional handful of men—either actual military soldiers, or dressed as soldiers for purposes of costumed fun—emerged from the conveyance as well. This was, evidently, the governor's retinue.

King Temm actually tried to ban the custom of "retinues"—bands of followers who travel with the powerful or famous—on Saurius Prime. But there are still those at home who follow the powerful in hopes it will rub off on them. Certainly the same is bound to be true in a species as volatile as human mammals, on a planet as unpredictable as Earth Orange.

Governor Claiborne grabbed my face.

"Ouch!" I said. "No derma-tugs, please! It's uncalled for!"

"What kind of accent is that, boy? You think you're clever keeping that costume on? We'll get it off. We'll figure out who you belong to."

Costume? Did he mean my chrono-suit, which was indeed looking a bit tattered? And what is this strange notion humans have of one life form *belonging* to another?

"Here is our problem, Mr. President," Governor Claiborne said, pointing to the fused mass that used to be my time-vessel. "Some kind of voodoo shrine bringing the runaway slaves out here. Here's that 'doorway' they've been using."

I thought this perhaps would be my chance to explain to everyone that what we were witnessing were side effects of plasmechanical technology becoming infected with local slow pox. Indeed, I wanted to warn everyone to be careful, since I hadn't established whether the biomechanical material was capable of spreading the disease to its local surroundings. Somehow, the combination of slow pox's cellular reproduction mechanism, crossed with the molecular replication aspects of the vessel itself, have caused this new, highly advanced Saurian ship to fuse with the landscape.

Its time-displacement features had somehow ruptured, creating local time vectors of uncertain calibration. In other words, it had created a large-scale time-sphere. Through which people were evidently disappearing.

Too many people time-traveling all at once, from the same historical moment, could have very wide-ranging and unpredictable consequences.

And I don't believe anyone on Earth Orange is prepared to deal with such consequences. After all, on their planet, time-voyaging was only recently discovered, by Eli's parents and Thea's mother at their respective junctures in history. It's still so new for them.

Concurrent with these field hypotheses, I noticed a dog mammal digging furiously in the vicinity of my ship, and I was worried it might slip into the vessel's sphere of influence and disappear into the time stream, too.

The dog was barking excitedly about something it was uncovering.

I tried to talk to it in wolfish, but the effect was to startle the dog, all the other dogs nearby, and most of the humans.

Governor Claiborne gave my face another derma-tug. "Somebody get this costume off!" he yelled.

The one named Jefferson came up to me, holding his own torch, and regarded me with intense curiosity.

"What if it's not a costume?" he said. Then he gave me his own derma-tug, pulling my cheek skin out, like a nest full of grandmames, clucking over hatchlings. "What if it's an *incognitum*?"

Further local meteorological disruptions flashed and sounded just then.

"Sir! Sir!" The one named Howard was trying to get Jefferson's attention. "The only discovery here is that there's been a *conspiracy*! Led by your own Sally—along with that runaway girl, Brassy!" He was pointing at Thea and her friend.

"How do you explain *this*?" Jefferson asked, pointing at me.

"Frankly, sir," Howard went on, "up until a few moments ago, I wasn't entirely sure anyone else saw it. It's something of a relief that you do."

"Can't we just let these wretches go back to

their owners, then be done with it?" Jefferson asked. Still looking at my face, he asked me, in a tongue different from English—the Latin, I think, that Thea has been known to use—"What exactly are you?"

"I am a student who is somewhat over-whelmed by his research," I replied.

Jefferson stepped back in surprise upon my reply. Then he said, "Well that makes two of us."

"We need to make examples of them, Mr. President," Governor Claiborne insist-droned. "We have to let it be known that your new Louisiana territory will not be soft on slavery."

My friends Eli and Thea were bound in the chains apparently used on the "slave" class. I had allowed myself to be similarly caught and bound earlier when it became apparent that any kind of skirmish or disruption might lead to weapons-discharge with a high, immediate flesh-rendering and deep ouch-factor, and I would not wish that on my friends.

As I stood, attempting to finish my conversa-tion with nest leader Jefferson, someone else was brought into camp and chained, as well. It was the one known as Howe. Upon catching sight of me, he burst into laughter, raised his chained fist, and shook it at me. He was holding a *sklaan*.

A *sklaan*!

The last *sklaan* I'd seen was the one Thea had in the time-vessel, the one she'd given away at the terrible factory cave. That was another place built upon the strange idea of human mammals owning one another.

Howe kept up his fevered laugh, all the time waving the *sklaan* at me. Apparently chronological displacement had not gone well for him.

Thea was then roughly separated from Eli and brought over with Sally.

"Hello once more, K'lion," she said.

"Who is teaching all these foreign languages to slaves!?" Governor Claiborne screamed. "And why is that man's costume still on?"

"These two," Howard said. "Brassy and Sally. You have to make examples of them."

"You have to be strong, Tom," Governor Claiborne declared. "The strength of the republic's at stake."

"I worry for a republic whose strength is based on keeping slaves," Jefferson said.

"You keep yours," Sally pointed out to him.

"Would you have left me, Sally? Were you going to run away?"

"I'm too famous, Jefferson. Where would I run to?"

"Potentially anywhere," I said, pointing to the time vector surrounding the ruins of my ship. "Considering the vast expanse of time in which none of us is known at all."

"That's what happens there, when you step through the doorway?" Sally asked, raising her chained hands toward the ship.

"It is my best theory. A temporal disruption caused by an unforeseen biomechanical reaction caused by a local disease vector. Though I am somewhat bereft of field equipment to fully test it."

The dog who had been digging by the time-vessel started barking again.

Governor Claiborne was talking—barking, too, really—at Thea.

"My wife's been missing you for months.

How could you do this to us?" He held up a torch, close to her face. "And how come you look different? Will somebody make that dog shut up?"

He spun around, fluster-bothered.

"I believe it's trying to tell us something," Jefferson said. "Look."

He leaned down and reached into the hole. He pulled out a pair of muddy bones. Then he extracted a stained silver chain, which revealed, after he knocked off the dirt, a piece of wrought, metal-smithed jewelry affixed to the end.

He looked at the bones closely, then set them down very carefully, as if he had new respect for them.

"Perhaps somebody here would like to say a prayer," he said. "I believe these are human."

Governor Claiborne wasn't looking at the mammal bones, however. He was transfixed by the small chain. He held it up to the torch flame.

"Look." He was holding up the locket. "A silver crescent. A symbol of New Orleans. There used to be a small green stone in the middle."

"How do you know?" Jefferson asked.

"Because," the nest-governor said, studying

the small, smithed piece of jewelry on both sides, "I recognize it. My wife gave it to Brassy. As a gift, because she"—he turned to look at Thea, then back at the hole in the ground—"she had grown fond of the girl, even though she was a slave. You're not Brassy," he said to Thea.

"No," Thea said.

"That's Brassy down there," the governor stated, to no one in particular. "She didn't get very far after all. Then who *are* you?" he asked Thea.

Human mammals, it appears, struggle often with the idea of who they might be, and who everyone else might be.

"I am Thea," she said in Eli's tongue. "Hypatia's daughter."

That's when Jefferson made his comment about surprises and bone trails.

And that's when I knew we had found our link. I hypothesized that if the ship had been here before Brassy's escape, then she may have made it into the time stream somewhere. But something happened to her. She perished, and her perishing could have been the very thing to alter history, drawing my time-ship to it when it tumbled out of the Fifth Dimension, and creating a—

"Prime nexus!" I called out.

"Is that a signal?" Howard asked suspiciously. "Watch those slaves!"

"Prime nexus! The one named Brassy! That's why the ship was drawn here, to this place, to this time!"

"What do you mean, K'lion?"

"Her early sad death changed everything! Had she not died while trying to escape, had she lived—I do guesswork here, but there is science to back me up—she would have had some tremendous role to play here on Earth Orange! A whole different history would have unfurled!"

"You mean, she would have *changed* history? How, Clyne?" Eli wondered.

"We shall never know. But all the equipment on the ship, sensitive to great time disruptions, was drawn to this spot. This grave."

"Our little Brassy," Governor Claiborne exclaimed, "was going to be . . . important? *Necessary?* What the hell are you saying, boy? And why won't that mask come off?"

I was about to make another potentially agitating observation, when Banglees walked into the clearing, carrying a wrapped bundle.

"Just whose side are you on, anyway?" Eli asked.

"Whoever pays me," he responded. "Whoever's ahead."

And so the attention of the human mammals shifted again. This all happened in the past few moments as I was still trying to get them to understand that a prime-nexus spot must be preserved for further research and examination.

But either no one here agrees with me, or they're just not focused on their studies.

Chapter Twenty-three

Eli: Vanishing Tale

February 1805

The last rocket of the night explodes in the sky, back in the direction of New Orleans, crackling with sparks of red and blue.

At least, it feels like the last one. There's a tremendous silence after the sparks fade from the sky. There isn't even any more thunder and lightning.

Maybe this is my chance to tell Thomas Jefferson the truth about this whole situation. If I did, maybe he'd help us out. Wasn't he the president who believed in honesty, anyway? The one with the cherry tree?

"I think we need to make some arrests," Claiborne says.

"He looks like Serapis," Thea whispers to me, pointing to his snake costume. "I had no idea the Alexandrian gods would last so long, considering how determined Tiberius was to destroy them."

"Mere arrests? We must *burn* this voodoo shrine, Mr. President," Howard says. "We must stamp out all vestiges of this conspiracy, and then let it be known that your firm hand was behind it."

Jefferson gives a big sigh. "Sometimes, I can scarcely wait to *not* be president, and retire full-time to Monticello."

Howard picks up another torch from one of the soldiers, so he has one in each hand. He starts walking toward the crash site of Clyne's ship.

"Arlington Howard! I order you once again to *stand down*!"

Jefferson's voice is loud and booming, in contrast to the laughter coming from Mr. Howe.

"*Arlington* Howard! You even got his name right!" Mr. Howe jumps in front of Jefferson. If his hands weren't chained up like the rest of ours, I think he might have grabbed him by the throat.

"Are you in on it?" he asks Jefferson, then Claiborne. "Are you? Are *you*?" He looks at Thea, then rattles his chains at me.

I couldn't rattle back, though, even if I wanted to. My hands are bound tight, and on top of it all, the packet of portable soup that Lewis gave me is leaking all over the place now, dripping inside my jacket and sleeves. The whole thing makes me realize that I probably need a really, really good bath.

"*Arlington* Howard!" Howe shouts. "Have you tried on the hat yet?"

Howard narrows his eyes suspiciously. "What hat?"

"The one that made you crazy!"

Howard's eyes narrow even more.

"Oh, this is all a test, isn't it? Some kind of elaborate holographic re-creation. Is it to find out if I'm still *loyal*? Is that it?"

Who is he talking to? Who else does he think is listening? He's obviously been back here awhile, but hasn't accepted it yet. And he looks terrible. I almost feel sorry for him.

"All the files you kept from me! You already *knew* about an 'M. Sands' who worked on a secret time-travel project during World War Two—and disappeared. The same project was taken over by a 'Dr. Royd' right after the war. You knew all this *before* you ever assigned me to be Sandusky's handler!"

Disappeared again? *Mom?* Where was she now? And what's a "handler"?

"The man is touched, sir!" Howard points at Mr. Howe. "And dangerous."

"And you, *you*, Mr. Arlington *Howard.* The family had to shorten its name after you vanished."

"Vanished!?" Howard looks startled. "Where? When?"

"Because you were busy helping slaves escape when you were supposed to be the Treasury agent protecting the president!"

"What!? Never!"

"That's the story that's been passed down from generation to generation."

"Why, Mr. Howard, I didn't know you had it in you," Sally says to him.

"I don't. I won't!"

"But Mr. Howe, shouldn't you be proud of him if he really helped slaves?" I ask.

Mr. Howe's eyes narrow. "Oh, yes, ask me a question and *test* me, *Danger Boy*. That story was a cover. I mean, who kept records of federal employees in 1800? Who *cared*? But you might, if the only trace of someone who deserts their post is a set of clothes—and *this*."

Mr. Howe waves the shimmering cloth at me.

"The *sklaan*!" Clyne chirps. "Plasmechanical extra skin, for moderating temperature extremes. Nicely engineered. Once used by Thea."

"The same material. Arlington Howard disappeared—"

"I did not!" Howard protests.

"—and all that was found were some of his clothes, and a snippet of this . . . this *alien* material, with cellular and molecular structures not found anywhere on Earth. It was stored in a restricted archive they didn't want me to see. But they retrieved the sample after they found this"—

and he shakes the *sklaan* again—"in Europe a few years ago. And because my distant ancestor was found with this same cloth on him, I find that *I* am a suspect. *I* am studied because perhaps I am something other than what I claim to be!"

"The *sklaan* is not meant for causing disruptions," Clyne says. "Only comfort."

"Comfort! Did *Danger Boy's* father steal this from my office in order to *comfort* somebody?"

"Hmmm, intriguing," Clyne continues. "Did Sandusky-sire say what he did take it for?"

"What for? Because you want to cut me out! You want me to be the last to know! Thirty! Sandusky! I don't know who or how or why, but I won't take the fall for this! I won't be set up! I want to keep my security clearance!"

"That is quite a fever-dream of a story, sir," Jefferson tells him. "What, pray, is 'security clearance'?"

"And what manner of man are you?" Howard asks.

"*Me?* You're just a hologram in some kind of elaborate test I'm going through! Why don't you ask about *him*"—he lifts his chains and points to

Clyne—"since he's an alien trying to invade the planet! Or *her*"—he points to Thea—"since she's some kind of witch or priestess from Egypt. Or *him*." He points to me. "Ask him why *Danger Boy* keeps putting everyone else at risk by not doing *exactly what we tell him to!*"

So that's it. Basically, Mr. Howe is upset with me because I don't do what I'm told. What about all the risk *I'm* in? What about the fact that I don't really have a family anymore?

Heck. Mr. Howe apparently has more family, at the moment, than I do.

"Your man is right, Mr. President. This fellow's touched. As are they all. Including, I'm afraid, your Mr. Howard. Let's just burn this site and get the soldiers to march everyone back to town." It's Claiborne again. He seems to be getting a little nervous himself. And the slaves, who'd been trying to escape, seem to be scared and angry. They're shifting around a lot, and they're making the soldiers and the farmers—the ones with the weapons—jittery as well.

"And to what *hat* did you refer?" Howard asks again. He seems to be taking it personally.

"Perhaps this hat?" Banglees says casually. "He was trying to bury it by the river when they caught him." He points to Mr. Howe. "I jus' dug it up."

He tosses a muddy blob of cloth down on the ground. Then he takes out a big buck knife and peels the material back.

And there, dirty and wet, but still in one piece, is my Seals cap.

Chapter Twenty-four

Eli: Closed Loop
February 1805

Banglees slams his knife through it.

"Do not touch it. It 'as strange powers, I think."

I look at Howe and his shredded clothes. He must have torn off pieces of his jacket to wrap around the hat. But if he's had it with him or near him, the whole time, how has it affected him?

"I was trying to keep it safe!" Howe shouts to no one in particular. "I wasn't going to use it! Isn't that part of the test!?"

"He must have wound up in possession of it," Thea tells me, her voice quiet but urgent, "when he and I fell through time together. I'm sorry."

"It's not your fault," I tell her. She lifts the chains to brush her fingers against my hand, to thank me, I guess, or let me know it's okay. It's a little bit corny, too—though not like that kiss—and I don't know if I should brush her back because that portable soup is running down my arm and out my sleeve, and I'd get it all over her, and then she'd feel greasy . . .

Greasy.

I start to move my wrist inside the irons. The soup is making my arm slippery.

"Give me the hat!" Howard yells. He leaps at Banglees, who grabs it up and twirls it on the end of his knife.

"For a price, perhaps. Remember, I 'ad to find it."

My poor Seals cap. "Hey, be careful, there's a Joe DiMaggio autograph inside!"

Everyone looks at me like they're going to add me to the "crazy" list.

"We need to put this place to the torch, Mr.

President," Claiborne insists again. "We need to master this situation with a firm hand."

The weeping and restlessness of the escaped slaves is now all mixed together. They don't know what's going to happen to them. They're frightened for their lives. It's almost like I can feel what they're feeling.

Know.

No what? *Know* what? Who's talking? Why is my lingo-spot itching so much? "Know what?" I say out loud, without really intending to.

Jefferson, at least, doesn't look at me like I'm nuts. In fact, he nods.

"The young squire is right, governor. We need to know exactly what mysteries we're facing here. What drove the slaves to this spot. What science possesses this lad's strange headgear. And where on earth this *incognitum* comes from." Jefferson paces around while he talks, and he winds up standing directly in front of Clyne.

"Not from this Earth, mammal man."

Jefferson looks around. "I think the enigmas we face here are much greater than the question of why slaves are escaping. We know why slaves escape." He looks at the faces around him in the torch light. "But we do not know what that strange apparatus is." He waves his hand at Clyne's ship. "Or how the bones of Brassy came to be buried here. Or how the *incognitum* came to know her."

"I do not know her! I just *tk-tk* deduce! She was a prime nexus! She had a history-changing *snkt* life ahead. But that was stolen from her. Everything changed *knkt!* on this spot."

"Changed, you say, *incognitum?* For the better, or . . . ?"

"Or for much more long-term sadness. It's unknown *sktkt!* until your history works itself out."

"Maybe, Tom," Sally says to Jefferson, "in Brassy's dying, there's a lesson. About the value of things. Of persons."

"You let her talk to you like that?" Claiborne asks.

"I think," Jefferson continues, sighing heavily, "we need to arrange a way of keeping what happened here a secret. Until we can deduce what has transpired and what it means for America."

"Are you saying we need to act to protect national security, sir?"

"I'm a little uncomfortable with the broadness of that phrase, Mr. Howard. But perhaps, yes. And I would like to start by relieving you of your duties until we determine your involvement with these strange personages."

"No. *No!* You cannot do this to me! You will not! You *must* not!" Howard looks around, like he's cornered, trapped, though no one moves toward him. Instead, he moves toward Mr. Howe—his descendant. And snatches the *sklaan* out of his hand. "Setting me up to take the fall with this! No! A thousand times I tell you, no! I was the one trying to maintain order! Me! *Me!*" And with another shake of the *sklaan*, he turns and sprints away toward the river, disappearing into the darkness.

He was acting just like Mr. Howe. Or, at least, the way Mr. Howe always acted until he showed up here in New Orleans.

A couple of the soldiers turn to pursue him. "No," Jefferson says. "Desist. Let him run. We will look for him in the morning. He can't get far tonight. And we can't afford any more people getting lost."

"Closed loop," Clyne says.

"What, *incognitum*?"

"Closed loop. He has the *sklaan* now. So it can be found. And then hidden by your government. And brought back again. Closed loops. Prime nexuses. Temporal displacement. *Tk-tk-tng!* Much to discuss. All fascinating. Do you study such things?"

Howe stands, still a little surprised, looking at the spot where his distant relative disappeared into the trees. And then, much to my surprise, he turns to me. And isn't mad or hysterical about something.

"I don't want to end up like him, Eli. I don't want to disappear."

"None of us do."

"She didn't want to disappear, either." Thea nods toward Brassy's grave. "I wonder who she was? Or if we'll ever know."

"Maybe we do know," Howe says. "Maybe it's another secret file I haven't come across yet."

The whole time this is going on, I wiggle my soup-drenched wrist around more. And more. Until I almost have it—

And then I do. I have one of my wrists out of the iron. But I clench my hands together, so no one knows yet.

"So what am I to do with this hat?" Banglees waves it around on the tip of his knife. "Does anyone care to buy it from me?"

"That's government property," Jefferson tells him. "I am ordering you to hand it over."

"I think, right now, it ees private property."

"You heard the president!" Mr. Howe lunges at Banglees. The trapper steps back in surprise and flashes his knife at Mr. Howe without thinking. Howe steps to the side, but the knife just catches him on the shoulder.

My Seals cap goes flying.

"Guards! Guards!" The governor is frantically calling his men over. After the fidgety slaves, Mr. Howard's dash into the woods, and the fight between Banglees and Mr. Howe breaking out, none of the soldiers is sure what to do, but a couple run toward us.

Clyne, who had been trying to avoid making sudden moves, so that the armed men wouldn't get too nervous, now jumps back and forth near his ship. "Watch out for the time sphere! Watch out for the *gng!* sphere!"

"Put it to the flame, Mr. President!" Governor Claiborne grabs one of the torches, using the distraction to start lighting leaves and branches near Clyne's ship. There's smoke, and the slow lick of flames.

The cap, meanwhile, has landed near the feet of Sally Hemings. She looks at me. She looks at Thea. Then she picks up a stick and uses it to toss the hat in Thea's direction.

"Is it part of the key," she asks, "to the doorway?"

I nod. Thea is reaching down to pick up the hat.

"Don't, Thea! Don't touch it!" I yell.

Howe and Banglees are still fighting. Howe uses his wrist irons to swing at Banglees. The knife has been knocked away, and the trapper's trying to get it back.

With the spreading fire, some of the slaves have jumped to their feet. "Halt!" Claiborne yells.

And then to the soldiers: "Do not fire until you hear my order!"

"No firing! No firing!" Jefferson yells back.

In the growing melee, a soldier knocks Thea down into the mud and is about to kick her. That's when I raise my arms. I jump toward Thea and shove the surprised soldier out of the way. He gets knocked back a few feet and crashes into the equally surprised Banglees.

I pull Thea up from the ground and, with my free hand, reach for the cap.

"Clyne!" I yell. "Let's go!"

"Wait!" Jefferson pleads. "Do not leave!"

Howe staggers over to me and collapses as he grabs my ankle. "Must protect Danger Boy. . . . Can't let anything else go wrong. . . ."

"Don't let them escape!" the governor shouts. "Stop them!" Some of the soldiers aim their guns at us.

Banglees has picked up his knife and is going to throw it at me.

Clyne's tail knocks the blade back out of Banglees's hand.

"*Zut alors!*"

"Fire!" Claiborne screams.

"Do *not* fire!" Jefferson yells back. "That is an order!"

It looks like one of the soldiers is intending to listen to the governor rather than the president. He sights us down his rifle.

The sky isn't quiet anymore. There's the crackle of more lightning in the air.

The soldier begins to squeeze the trigger.

Then Sally steps in front of him, blocking his view of us.

The soldier stops, confused, releases his finger, and looks to the governor, then to Jefferson, to figure out what to do next.

That gives Clyne enough time to jump over to us. I pull Thea closer. Howe's fingers are locked on my ankle.

"Never chrono—*zzzp!*—traveled without a ship before! Hope it—"

I put the cap on my head. It's torn and dirty, but I still feel the tingling.

"—works!"

I see the lights of the Fifth Dimension begin to swirl around me, replaced by colors that grow longer and longer . . .

. . . as the world of Lewis, Clark, North Wind Comes, Thomas Jefferson, Sally Hemings, Kentuck, and Gassy disappears.

My friends are still holding on to me and I won't let go of them.

And this time, wherever we're headed, we'll get there together.

ACKNOWLEDGMENTS

You're now holding an all-new Danger Boy story—the first I've written in a little while. The telling of this tale has been a journey of its own—and a pleasure. And as the stories in these books widen to include ever more people, so do the thank-yous. Which is to say, everyone previously thanked should consider themselves still gratefully acknowledged, for their patience, love, good wishes, and all other kinds of support.

More specifically, this time out, I'd like to acknowledge the genealogical inspiration of my history-researching cousin, Paula Bynum; the trans-species linguistic skills of Clyne fan Daniel Branch, whose additional thoughts about Saurian language were both helpful and inspirational; Daniel Slosberg, who re-creates the character and music of Pierre Cruzatte and whose knowledge of the Corps of Discovery, and Cruzatte in particular, was enormously valuable; Naida and Patrick Graham for the many Medici-like ways they support their local scribes; and barrister Stephen J. Strauss for help and spark-lighting on the practical side of being a writer.

And, of course, the entire gang at Candlewick, especially my editor, Monica Perez, who is both insightful and—at deadline time—somewhat long-suffering.

See you all along the trail.

Mark London Williams lives in Los Angeles, where he writes books, comics, plays, and a regular column in which he tries to make sense of Hollywood. He continues to draw inspiration from his two sons and one old dog, and particularly thanks his oldest son, Elijah, for running down the hall one day when he was little and yelling, "I'm a Danger Boy!"

About this book, the author says "I've always wanted to write about Lewis and Clark and their epic travels—since long before they became famous all over again! For better and worse, their journey changed the history of America—the very stuff that the Danger Boy books are all about. And it was fun being on the trail with them, just a little bit, while this story was being written."

Eli's adventures continue in Episode 4

Danger Boy
City of Ruins

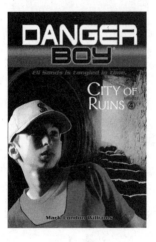

"This looks and feels a little like Alexandria," Thea tells me. Then in English, "But more freeze."

She shudders. But not from the cold. She's burning up. From fever.

This place is a little like Alexandria. There are stone buildings—or there were—no street lamps, and no electricity. The setting sun is our only source of light. And from what I can see, it looks like an earthquake just rolled through the place.

An excerpt from *City of Ruins: Danger Boy Episode 4*

A lot of the buildings have caved in or been knocked down. And it smells like there's been a fire. Ash and smoke are all mixed with a thin layer of snow—the "freeze" Thea mentioned.

People are picking through the ruins, and they're dressed a lot like the people in Alexandria: robes, or shawl-kinds-of-things wrapped around them. Except a lot of the robes seem to be falling apart, too thin for snow. And it seems not everyone could afford a pair of sandals either.

"Is this Yeru-sha-layem?" Thea asks. She says it differently, even through the lingo-spot.

"Yeah, Jerusalem. I hope so," I tell her.

A woman shuffles by us, staring. She's wrapped up against the cold but peers out with deep eyes—deep the way a hollow log is deep. Like something has been scooped out of her.

"Philadelphians," she hisses, then speeds up as she goes by us.

What? She thinks we're from Philadelphia?

And even if we were, what's wrong with that? The A's came from there, originally. Wait, no. "Philistines," the lingo-spot tells me.

An excerpt from *City of Ruins: Danger Boy Episode 4*

What's a Philistine?

Near the top of the hills, where the ruins seem to have belonged to a palace—maybe it had a library in it, too, like Thea's museum home in Alexandria—there's a line forming.

Men, women, and kids—mostly women and kids, the ones who aren't picking through rubble everywhere else—are standing in a long line waiting . . .

Waiting to see a woman, who's sitting near one of the pillars that hasn't fallen over. I can't see what she looks like; with the sun behind her, she's just a silhouette.

I wonder if she's some kind of doctor or mayor. Or, since this looks like it might be a pretty religious time, a priest or a rabbi.

That is, if women were allowed to be any of those things.

"She's Gehanna-marked," she says, pointing to Thea. The other people turn to look at us.

These people don't seem too happy we're here. The woman who accused us of being from Philadelphia tries to get as far away from us as possible without losing her place in line.

An excerpt from *City of Ruins: Danger Boy Episode 4*

"What does she mean?" Thea asks. I'm so used to her being, well, pretty much smarter than me, that the question surprises me. But more and more, since she's been affected with slow pox, I find myself explaining things to her. When I can.

"I don't know what it means," I tell her. Though I'm guessing it has something to do with others being able to recognize the effects of the disease on her, even in this half-light.

"No more Gehanna-*spawn," someone else says. "We've suffered enough."*

"No more Gehanna-*spawn!"*

Everyone's eyes have that hollow look, like they've all seen too many things they wished they hadn't.

"Back to Gehanna with her then!"

"Back with both of them!" That's a kid's voice. A boy. I see him reaching for a rock.

Maybe this place is more like Alexandria than I realized.

The line breaks up as people start to surround us. Thea's not in any shape to start running.

An excerpt from *City of Ruins: Danger Boy Episode 4*

"No," a commanding voice says. "No."

It's the woman who everyone's been waiting to see.

The hollow-eyed people move away to give her room.

"No. We are all Gehanna-marked now, one way or another."

The woman's head is wrapped in scarves, too, which get lost in the yellow and blue robes around her. Dark curly hair, with streaks of gray in it, spill out and surround her face. Her eyes don't look like hollow logs, though you can tell she's still one of those grown-ups who've seen too many sad things, the kinds of things that are impossible to explain to kids.

"My name's Huldah," she says.

Since she doesn't have a lingo-spot, as far as I know, she wouldn't be able to understand anything I'd tell her. But I guess I should try.

"This is Thea," I tell her, pointing to my sweaty, shivering friend. "And she's not from Gehanna at all, wherever that is." And then I point to myself. "And I'm—"

An excerpt from *City of Ruins: Danger Boy Episode 4*

"Eli," Huldah finishes for me. "You are Eli. We've been expecting you. I'm glad you're finally here."

Somebody's been waiting for me?

Here in ancient Jerusalem?